Missouri

Missouri

CHRISTINE WUNNICKE

Translated by David Miller

Arsenal Pulp Press | Vancouver

Originally published as *Missouri*, © 2006 MännerschwarmSkript Verlag

MISSOURI
by Christine Wunnicke
Translation copyright © 2010 by David Miller

ARSENAL PULP PRESS
Suite 200, 341 Water Street
Vancouver, BC
Canada V6B 1B8
arsenalpulp.com

Mixed Sources
Cert no. SW-COC-001271
© 1996 FSC

FSC

The translation of this work was supported by a grant from the Goethe-Institut, which is funded by the German Ministry of Foreign Affairs.

Book design by Shyla Seller
Cover photograph copyright © Denver Public Library, Colorado Historical Society, and Denver Art Museum

Printed and bound in Canada on 100% PCW recycled paper

Library and Archives Canada Cataloguing in Publication

Wunnicke, Christine, 1966-
        Missouri / Christine Wunnicke ; translated by David Miller.

Translation from the German of novel with same title.
ISBN 978-1-55152-344-6

        I. Miller, David, 1956 Jan. 8- II. Title.

PT2685.U56M5813 2010   833'.92   C2010-900549-X

I

I T WAS IN HUMBLE LODGINGS in Manchester's Great
Ancoats Street that court reporter Douglas Fortescue
dyed his hair black in August 1832 and decided to reform English poetry.

Following instructions gleaned from *Fashionable Life,* he
had concocted a mixture of slaked lime and extract of coal tar;
having previously rinsed with chlorinated water, he now carefully brushed the sticky paste onto his exceedingly sleek and
shoulder-length hair, strand by strand.

It was high time to get rid of the tiresome ash blond. It reminded Douglas of Yorkshire, of fresh air, of too many meals,
of a clan of lusty peasantry to whom the young Fortescue had
the great misfortune to be related. It also reminded him of his
brother Jeremy, who still lived in Yorkshire and who would—
without the necessary assistance—remain blond until the
end of his days. Douglas pondered whether he should post
him a strand of black hair if the experiment were to prove

successful. Jeremy disapproved of his little brother's fanciful notions. He frowned upon his being in Manchester. He would rather have had him in Yorkshire, where he, widowed at an early age, was preparing his four children for adult life. This, he considered, was something his brother might likewise find beneficial. When he was done, Douglas wrapped a towel around his head, knotted it into a turban, and with a faint smile wiped the tarry brush on a copy of Byron's *Childe Harold*.

Byron was dead. Byron's throne was vacant. Nobody matched Lord Byron's erstwhile fame; Douglas Fortescue had to rectify this sorry state of affairs. He allowed himself no more than two hours to devise his plan of action, precisely the time recommended by *Fashionable Life* for the tar extract to take effect. Douglas was twenty-two years old, and as far as becoming famous was concerned, he was gradually losing his patience.

He abhorred poetry. He abhorred poets. He saw them as wretchedness personified, defenseless creatures tormented by love and hate and visions, poisoned by laudanum and hysteria. Poets felt. And felt. And felt. A chill ran down Douglas's spine as soon as he thought about poets. Occasionally, whenever he forced himself to read their works in order to familiarize himself with the forms poetry assumed, his hand jerked involuntarily to the smoked-glass spectacles in his waistcoat pocket, to his shield against the malign intrusiveness of the world. Douglas Fortescue the court reporter had spent a good month's salary on this adornment. The dark glasses made it easier for him to coexist with human beings, yet they offered no succor against poetry.

His scalp itched as he leafed through his collection of court transcripts. He always kept the shorthand version when he submitted the fair copy to the chief clerk. Douglas read the squabbling about legacies, claims, and embezzlement, the clamor of factory owners in this or that dispute with their debtors. He read the deranged rantings of an innkeeper from Huddersfield who had done wicked things with his wife's corpse. He skimmed the lamentation of a maiden aunt who had taken care of her sister's children, latterly with arsenic. Slowly Douglas leafed through the life and confessions of an Irish thief, whom he recalled as a glimmer of light in his otherwise dreary life as a recordkeeper: freckles, broad shoulders, broad hands—far too big, like a puppy's paws—his shirt wrongly buttoned in his agitation, and a tuft of red chest hair bursting forth. Douglas quickly turned the page; singing the praises of youthful thieves was certainly not the road to Mount Parnassus.

Douglas allowed himself no favorites. Douglas Fortescue was even-handed. They all passed in front of his eyes, one after the other, agitated and close to tears, the heirs and the disinherited, the victims and the perpetrators, the elderly little chap with the goatee beard who had misappropriated funds, the innkeeper, the spinster, the thief, and all the Manchester cotton barons in their sweat-stained silk shirts, verging on apoplexy. What did they have in common? They suffered. They struggled for words. They felt. And felt. Douglas adjusted his turban and grinned. It was so simple. A legion of poets had passed in front of him and he hadn't even noticed. Douglas laughed. He had devised a new laugh for himself, weak and unattractive, with a slight ring to it. He already had it down to a fine art.

A quarter of an hour before the dye was ready, Douglas Fortescue resolved to base his reform of English poetry on a court report. Five minutes later it was evident to him that the world should remain ignorant of this source of inspiration. Then he decided: no rhymes. Because rhymes, Douglas opined, were tedious and antiquated.

He removed the towel from his head, thoroughly rinsed out the dye, drew a parting in the middle, and combed his hair over his cheeks and down to his shoulders. Then he stood in front of the mirror. It was a success. His hair was black as night, with a certain tinge of ginger that *Fashionable Life* had already cautioned him about. He carefully let his hair glide through his fingers. It felt strange, unnatural, a novel material, created in some factory.

Douglas suppressed a vague disgust. Then he said, "A-ha." He sucked in his cheeks and raised his eyebrows. It was the deuce of a job turning this face into the face of a poet. Year in, year out, Douglas fought against the legacy of Yorkshire. He avoided the sun and dined upon vinegared potatoes. Douglas had the same broad jaw as Jeremy, the identical short nose, and he was tall like Jeremy, far too athletic, far too hirsute. "A-ha," repeated Douglas. He wished he could purchase a face in a shop, one as perfect as the smoked-glass spectacles. He wished he were Doctor Frankenstein, and yet his own monster too. Occasionally, in moments of weakness, he yearned for a knight's armor: three layers of iron plates and a helmet with a riveted visor. Douglas looked into Douglas's eyes. The eyes pleased him. They were green, very green. He couldn't have dyed them better. "Oh," said Douglas. He shaved carefully, first his cheeks, and then his chest.

Douglas Fortescue's debut, a poem of twenty-two pages, appeared in London at the end of 1832. It made its author famous overnight. It was seized, banned, examined by experts, released again, reviewed, and banned once more, which further increased sales. The title was *Thirst*. It dealt with blood and a woman named Claire. It was a little hard to understand. The ladies detected the whiff of vampires. The journals, depending on their outlook, revealed it to be an allegory of love, of modern-day depravity, or of Manchester's industrial squalor. The English poets, led by Mr Wordsworth, gathered on the verdant shores of Lake Windermere to found a short-lived society for the preservation of rhyme. "Oh, children," sighed Douglas. "How passé!"

In two nights, increasingly plagued by heartburn, he had committed his work to paper. It comprised the confession of the deranged innkeeper from Huddersfield who had slain his Claire with a meat cleaver and then, in desperation, eaten her bit by bit. This was enriched with statements from neighbors and the local constabulary. Douglas had shaken and stirred all of this and rearranged it in an agreeable manner.

> *Purple and wet*
> *Her little heart*
> *And I squeezed it out like grapes*
> *And we were married*
> *Oh, married before God and men.*

It was hardly surprising, thought Douglas, that such activity should provoke the gastric juices; nonetheless, he gladly accepted this in exchange for fame.

"A dream," said the poet Fortescue whenever people pressed him hard at the capital's soirées and salons, "nothing but a dream about *la dolce vita.*" He said no more. He sucked in his cheeks, adjusted the smoked-glass spectacles, and uncomplainingly allowed himself to be ogled. He trusted the public. The public would understand *Thirst.* Because a poem's value, realized Douglas Fortescue, not without amazement, is gauged solely by the reader whom it delights.

II

ROUGHLY FIFTEEN MILES downstream from New
Harmony on the Wabash River was the place they
called the Bone Bank. It had once been a ceme-
tery whose remains, pottery shards, and bleached
bones still graced the dusty riverbank. In August 1832, it was
on this bend of the Wabash that Joshua Jenkyns shot his first
man.

They had often passed this way before. Joshua didn't like
the bones. Father gave him a clip round the ear if he squeezed
his eyes tight shut. He knew when Joshua was squinting, even
though he was sitting behind him; this puzzled Joshua. "Eyes
open, Josh," ordered Father, "or else I'll be leaving you here."
Joshua didn't want Father to leave him there, somewhere in
the woods by the Wabash where the settlers were doubtless
awaiting their chance to roast the young son of the terrible
Cyrus Jenkyns over the fire. He wanted to stay with Father,

which was only right, so Josh Jenkyns opened his eyes and stared, sitting silently in front of Father in the saddle.

He saw many dead people. He saw white bones, decaying bodies here and there in the landscape, and while Father reloaded he saw the newly dead who lay in their own blood, a look of astonishment on their faces. It was all of a piece: the reloading, the blood, and the singular expressions of the dead. When Mother was still alive he had asked her what it was like to die, and Mother had replied that it was always the same. The dead went to their families and stayed there forever, arranged in accordance with their gender, importance, and date of death. Mother didn't explain any further. And when it was her turn to die she was gone, and maybe she was in hell, as Father maintained, or maybe she was with her family, as she herself had maintained, with the redskins and the spirits of her ancestors.

Cyrus Jenkyns thought it was about time for Josh, so he had captured a man in New Harmony, brought him to the Bone Bank, and tied him to a tree. Joshua was roughly six years old; nobody had taken the trouble to count. Cyrus Jenkyns lifted him from the horse and gave him a gun.

The men laughed. One look from Cyrus silenced them. He had trained his people well, so they dismounted and formed a semi-circle around the black-haired child with the slanting eyes for whom the gun was still far too big.

"I commend your soul to God," said Cyrus Jenkyns. "Shoot

that man dead, and if you do it with one bullet the gun's yours."

Joshua looked at the man by the tree. He looked at Father's beautiful gun in awe. "Cut him loose, sir. I'll give it a try," said Josh.

Cyrus laughed. "That does you credit, but he'll run if I untie him, so then you'll shoot him in the back, and that ain't no good either."

Joshua held the gun firmly in both hands. He had diligently practiced shooting at the settlers' wild pigs, which ran like the Devil, whereas the man by the tree sat totally still, and it was actually far too easy.

The captive looked at Joshua questioningly. He came from Boston. He had been meant to measure something hereabouts, but now he was waiting for a child to shoot him. The man from Boston couldn't understand that.

Joshua wished the prisoner would close his eyes, but he didn't. Joshua squinted. He suddenly no longer knew how to shoot. The gun was heavy. Joshua snuffled. "Hurry up, Josh," said Father. Joshua once more looked the captive in the eyes, and then he swallowed and pulled the trigger.

He couldn't do it with one bullet. His aim was poor. Three men lent Josh their weapons so that he wouldn't have to reload, and Josh needed four bullets before the man by the tree was no longer moving.

The men applauded all the same. Cyrus didn't stop them. He told his son to look in the dead man's coat pockets to see if they held anything of use. Joshua obeyed. He got his fingers bloody. There was only a handkerchief and a small thing made of leather and paper, which he took to his father.

"Oh, a book," said Cyrus contemptuously. "You've caught someone with a *book*."

Joshua examined the thing that Father called "book," and discovered that you could open it and that there was blood on the thing and that the leather spine was torn. A bullet had probably grazed the so-called book.

"Keep it," said Cyrus. "Maybe it'll bring you luck." And Cyrus Jenkyns shooed his men onto their horses and lifted Joshua onto his, and then he himself mounted and rode off. The man from Boston remained by the tree, and it wasn't long before his skeleton graced the banks of the Wabash, clean and white like the bones of yesteryear.

Joshua Jenkyns kept the book. Maybe he needed some luck in this life. Months passed before he dared ask the Professor for help. The Professor was called Professor because he could read, and Joshua wasn't allowed to talk to the Professor. The Professor was a kind of surgeon. Cyrus kept him because you often needed a surgeon in this line of business, but otherwise he chose to ignore him.

One night, Josh crawled on all fours to the Professor, held the book out to him, and asked: "Please, what is this?"

"A book," whispered the Professor. He didn't want Cyrus to catch him talking to the boy. Sure, Cyrus was asleep, but Cyrus never slept soundly.

"What kind?" breathed Joshua.

The Professor opened the book. He held it up to the fire and turned it until he could decipher the title page. "*Lord Byron, Collected Works, Volume Two.*"

"Thanks," whispered Joshua. "What's that?"

"Throw it into the fire, Josh."

"It's lucky!"

The Professor groaned.

"Read something," begged Joshua.

The Professor imagined what was likely to happen if Cyrus Jenkyns caught him reading to his son from a book. He wasn't keen to find out.

"Please," whispered Joshua.

The Professor shook his head.

"Just a little bit. Please!" Joshua became louder. The Professor was afraid someone might wake up. He opened the book in the middle and read two lines at random:

> *If solitude succeed to grief,*
> *Release from pain is slight relief*

And then he would read no more.

Joshua memorized the peculiar sentence. *If solitude succeed to grief* ... many things were easier now that Josh had the sentence. It was a mystery and a solace and a companion, and you could talk quietly to the sentence if nobody else wanted to speak to you.

Eventually he lost the book, but he was left with the sentence. He recited it in his head when he sat in front of Father in the saddle, and he was still saying it long after he'd been given his own horse. He celebrated the day he got his first gun and the day he got his first rifle with Byron at his side. He said the sentence while he was shooting, first at pigs and then at men. When Joshua was eleven, he noticed for the first time what fun it was to shoot at men, and his heart rejoiced. He chose the line from Lord Byron to accompany this too, because there was nothing else at hand.

Josh was a prodigy. When he was twelve he could shoot better than Cyrus. And when they then caught and hanged old Jenkyns on a hill near Decatur on the Sangamon River, the roughly fourteen-year-old Joshua came into his inheritance and got very drunk, full of joy and fear. He spurred himself on with eleven words from Byron, and as he was sometimes wont to do, he shouted a wordless cry into the vast, empty landscape, because Joshua liked this world and relished his chosen occupation, which in any case he had long ago mastered in a way Father never could.

If solitude succeed to grief ... Joshua suddenly found it boring. He fetched Decatur's priest from the cabin that served as a church and led him off, and when the priest finally stopped trembling he had to teach Josh Jenkyns how to read. An attentive student, with his rifle on his knees. The men didn't even dare to grin.

III

A-HA," SAID DOUGLAS FORTESCUE. Jeremy would gladly have boxed his ears. He said nothing but "a-ha," hour after hour. For seven years to be precise, ever since Jeremy had been living with his famous brother in London, managing his business affairs. The celebration marked Douglas's thirtieth birthday and the appearance of his new book, *The Waltz*. Initially he had wanted to call it *Chloroform*, but his publisher had objected. "A-ha," said Douglas, and sank once again into that exquisite rigidity which for some people indicated genius, for others a hint of the demoniacal, and for Jeremy nothing but absurd, excruciating cussedness. Douglas sat enthroned in his armchair like a pharaoh, one that was possibly already embalmed: pale, gaunt, his face frozen in a far-away smile. His blue-black hair hung neatly over the back of the chair, forming a smooth, shiny surface. Next to him on a little table stood the customary glass of milk; the illustrious author of *Thirst* subsisted on virtually nothing but milk—because, as he was fond of saying, his delicate stomach could only digest blood on special occasions.

Jeremy observed the revelers in disgust. They were in thrall to the German dance, spinning around in a wild and primitive fashion that was surely injurious to their health. The title of Fortescue's new book was no accident, since the incessant waltzing was a hallmark of his parties. No other dance made the guests so giddy, so poetical. Douglas Fortescue no longer had access to court proceedings, so was obliged to procure the necessary lunacy elsewhere; as ever, he was disinclined to poetize his own madness.

He held court in a palace of white marble, Greek friezes, and Sphinxes on the staircase—all loaned by a patron. It commanded a view of Regent's Park and the menagerie of the Zoological Society—an altogether suitable neighbor in Jeremy's eyes. He hated London. He hated Douglas's profession and his part in it. His eldest son attended school in Harrow whilst the little ones were entrusted to a woman of irreproachable character who ran a boarding establishment in Yorkshire. Jeremy wanted to spare his children the poet's household overlooking Regent's Park. For seven years he had been managing Douglas's assets. He disapproved of their origins, yet ultimately they funded Harrow and the children's boarding school, not to mention the fine coach in which

Jeremy paid visits to publishers, banks, and bountiful art lovers of every complexion. "Oh, what a blessing," said Douglas, "that I have you."

Jeremy drummed two fingers on the occasional table, stubbornly resisting the rhythm of the waltz. Douglas's milk vibrated gently. In the corners and alcoves, guests furtively sniffed at their handkerchiefs, swaying in ecstasy. The entire room was lightly perfumed with chloroform, the sickly-sweet American poison. "Keep your fingers still, Jeremy darling," said Douglas softly, "because otherwise you'll frighten my muse and the two of us will shortly be bankrupt." Jeremy snorted. Douglas smiled quietly to himself.

Douglas Fortescue was accustomed to calling approximately ten people "darling," his brother included. Jeremy was the only one to whom this privilege was granted in perpetuity; the others were favored for a season. They were mostly young men: hard-drinking, hard-dancing, prone to diverse bouts of delirium. They came from reputable families, something to which Douglas attached particular importance. He quietly observed his favorites, and quietly absorbed what they were saying, feeling, enjoying, and suffering. Their images faded when others took their place, whilst their words, honed to rhymeless beauty, were published to great pecuniary advantage. Madness had come naturally to the innkeeper from Huddersfield, whereas in London it now emanated from bottles and tins whose contents also tended to vary with the changing seasons. Chloroform was preceded by absinthe. Absinthe was preceded by laudanum. Laudanum was preceded by arsenic, though only for a fortnight. There was an unfortunate accident, and Douglas forbade it.

Prior to this, one imbibed "colors." Douglas still mourned its passing, and had speech not been so painful for him he would have been tempted to restore it to fashion. "Colors" was a blend of thorn apple and belladonna in brandy, created by chance during a botanical experiment. Douglas himself had christened it "colors." He gathered that drinking the mixture made one see colors, not to mention plants, animals, landscapes, and any manner of outlandish visions, sometimes charming, sometimes grotesque, soon wafting and melting away, and then once again so tangible that they seemed to be within reach. A few mouthfuls of "colors" had bestowed an entire river landscape on a young man called Donnie, whose name the poet had uncharacteristically remembered. At one fell swoop this gaudy panorama had engulfed the beautiful white marble staircase in Fortescue's palace: twisting vegetation and dusty black creatures framed a heavily silted stream full of flotsam, snakes, and roses. Stagnant and menacing, its muddy-brown water languished under a yellow-spotted and far too immense sky. The boy named Donnie had noisily eulogized his Acheron, and had thereupon fainted and been brought to his bed. The poet Fortescue had shaken his head, sipped at his milk, and then dashed off a book, his second success after *Thirst*. The critics choked upon Fortescue's brown river in all kinds of peculiar ways. There were literary quarrels in London, Paris, and New York. The author remained silent, or he sighed: "Colors, merely colors." The second and third impressions were soon printed. The book was called *Colors*, like the drug.

"Delightful," said Douglas Fortescue whenever he observed the lives of his darlings and listened to their versifying. "A-ha!" he said whenever Jeremy presented him with the accounts. "And yet, dearest brother, you still don't love me?" Douglas didn't expect any answer. He laughed his brittle laugh. Douglas Fortescue was impervious to worldly concerns, which fell away like the raindrops on his smoked-glass spectacles. Jeremy might harrumph, the *jeunesse dorée* might waltz ever so prettily, and an over-excited young lady might even forget herself and offer him her love, her honor, her dowry, or even her carotid artery, yet all of this affected Douglas Fortescue no more than the endless cries of the peacocks that rang out to him day and night from the enclosures of the Zoological Society.

Faster and faster went the waltz. The players were exhausted, and their increasing weariness made their fiddling wilder and wilder, spurring on the dancers as they spun in a three-step turn: Douglas Fortescue's well-oiled musical box. Everything was as usual on his thirtieth birthday: the waltz, the milk, Jeremy's distemper, the garrulous youths of exquisite pedigree. Even the spies were no strangers. They made an appearance at all of his parties as well as other occasions when only a few handpicked favorites were present in the salon. They were poorly dressed fellows, dispatched by anxious fathers or by Scotland Yard.

For eight years people had been watching and waiting, finally hoping to catch the poet out. A reviewer of *Thirst* had christened him "Fatal Fortescue" and the name had stuck, yet nobody, neither the fathers nor the police nor Jeremy, had ever witnessed the slightest lack of decorum. Green eyes, black hair, a reluctance to speak, and a penchant for mourning dress were not punishable; neither, indeed, were belladonna and laudanum. Fortescue never quarreled with anyone. He never permitted himself love affairs or duels. Scotland Yard grit its teeth and combed through his poems in the hope that they might betray him, but nothing that could expose Fatal Fortescue's sins had ever been entrusted to paper.

"Give me the poodle, darling," said Douglas to Lord Warrington's son, well within hearing of Lord Warrington's spy. Lord Warrington's son placed the poodle on Douglas's lap. "Thank you," said the poet. The young man knelt beside his armchair. Douglas stretched out his hand and momentarily caressed Lord Warrington's son behind the ear. Then he sighed and transferred his affections to the poodle. Lord Warrington's son giggled. Douglas stroked the poodle and gave Lord Warrington's spy a long, weary smile. It was likewise not punishable to caress Lord Warrington's chloroformed youngest behind the ear; Douglas Fortescue was certain of this.

"What do you do with the boys?" asked Jeremy, year in year out.

"Oh," Douglas invariably replied, "I merely drink their poisoned blood."

"Answer me," cried Jeremy. Douglas yawned. "Nothing, Jeremy. I do nothing with them. I observe them, and I might have the occasional thought if I happen to be in a philanthropic mood."

"And what are your thoughts?" asked Jeremy.

"I have none, darling. Who says that I'm ever in a philanthropic mood?"

And thus concluded this never-changing conversation.

Douglas Fortescue was now thirty years old, and his seventh book had appeared. A little fireworks display in his honor had been arranged in Regent's Park, where the air was rent by the screams of the monkeys and the cries of the peacocks from the nearby menagerie. "Let us drink to myself, the new era, and our joint contribution to the art of poetry," said Douglas. He clinked glasses with Lord Warrington's son, milk against champagne.

"This will turn out badly," whispered Jeremy once people were back inside.

"Badly?" asked Douglas. "Oh well."

I𝒱

O NCE HE HAD LEARNED to read, Joshua Jenkyns
restored the priest from Decatur to his church
and promptly ambushed the Northern Cross
Railway, not far from Meredosia.

He couldn't abide the puffing metal box which for no discernible reason rolled back and forth for ten miles across the prairie, so he rode up to the rails and waited. Two men had been left hanging with Father on the gallows. Three remained, and they had chosen to follow the son. Josh left the dead to the vultures.

It was a special day for Northern Cross. The Gregory brothers had bought the company, and were traveling on this stretch of track to celebrate the occasion. They were accompanied by ladies, a journalist from St Louis, and the sheriff of Jacksonville, all crammed into the locomotive because carriages hadn't yet been provided. The Gregorys were announcing their plans for the future: a railroad from Quincy right through to Lake Erie, and the best engines from Rogers & Ketchum. Corks popped, and they noisily toasted the new era; champagne trickled into their beaver collars.

Joshua's horse was standing motionless on the ties. At first, the fireman reckoned there must be some inanimate object blocking the way. Then he furrowed his brow. Then he dropped his shovel. "Lord protect us," cried the fireman. "That's the son of Cyrus Jenkyns' squaw!"

The locomotive braked, and before the sheriff of Jacksonville could find the trigger he realized he no longer had a gun, because Josh had fired and duly disarmed him without harming a hair on his head.

Joshua whistled to his men. He watched as they fetched the fireman from behind his boiler and a yellow-bellied Mr Gregory from behind a lady, and how they then assembled them all in front of the metal box and relieved them of what they had about their person: a little silver and a pearl necklace, hardly worth speaking about.

Joshua had dismounted to receive the loot, and now he reloaded and remounted, rifle in hand. He turned his horse. And if the journalist from St Louis had held his tongue, the annals would not only have recorded this ambush as the first railroad robbery west of the Alleghenies, but as the least bloody too. However, the journalist bent down to the lady at his side and whispered gravely: "You see, ma'am? A half-breed." And so Joshua was forced to turn around once more, whereupon he fired and the journalist keeled over. This is what Cyrus Jenkyns' son had learned: never let anyone call you a half-breed. And people could tell at first glance, because Cyrus's Scottish blood had fought a losing battle against the slanting eyes and shapely nose of the Omaha maiden whom Father had once bought for two gallons of firewater because he sought an heir for his business. The only thing Josh had from Father was his curls, and maybe the lice that prospered so well in them, and he had Father's men and Father's best rifle.

Joshua rode to Springfield. Father had avoided Springfield, but the vultures were eating Father, and Josh was a free man. He asked for Byron in Smith's General Store, and struck lucky despite this being no everyday request. Mr Smith, his nose somewhat out of joint, came across *Hours of Idleness* behind the Bibles, covered in dust. Joshua didn't hear the sheriff gathering his men outside. They cleared the street, shooing away the women and children. Joshua stood stock still, totally enamored of his book, deaf and blind to the world. He then had to shoot his way out. It was a black day in the history of Springfield.

Only gradually did it dawn upon Joshua that he could read, letter by letter, line by line. This discovery made him cry out loud. He frightened the men. He cried the peculiar cry he'd only dared give vent to since Father's death: joyful, bewildered, the cry for the prairie, for the angry people of Springfield, and for Josh's beloved *Hours of Idleness*. This extraordinary habit frightened everyone. It even frightened Josh himself. He didn't know why he did it. It sounded like an animal, like a creature without words—but sometimes, try as he might ... sometimes Joshua Jenkyns had to cry out loud.

He spent a year in Illinois and took whatever he could: a couple of pocket watches and some silver; Josh had modest ambitions. He didn't dream of a little farm as Father had done, even though he hadn't admitted it. He didn't need a squaw or a beaver hat. Joshua liked playing the game. He liked the small armies that pursued him, assembled by some sheriff or other and a motley collection of war veterans. He knew the land so well. It was fun to play here. So Joshua shouted and fired and people died, yet Joshua rode on, lousy, untamed, and immune to bullets. The bounty on his head was already earning interest.

Sometimes he rode into a town and watched the street empty. He searched for books but never found any. Sometimes he rented a whore for himself and his men. He paid in advance, and sat her behind him on his horse. The days spent with whores were unsettling. Their chatter spoilt Josh's fun. They talked, and sometimes wept too. Joshua would gladly have shut their mouths, but he didn't dare touch them, not on the face at any rate. He quickly passed them on to his men, who grunted and growled and wheezed like badgers that have been flushed out of their sett. Josh was sorely tempted to shoot them, and the whores too.

He rode out onto the plain, where he often remained alone for days on end. He lay in the grass and beguiled the idle hours with Byron. The words were full of mystery. The more you read them, the less you understood.

Sometimes Josh conversed with Lord Byron. He told him about his new gun, of which he was very proud. He had taken it from a traveler somewhere near Peoria City. It was a delicate handgun with five rounds and just one single barrel. Josh was crazy about it. He told the poet how slim it was, how it stored the bullets in a cylinder, how accurately it fired, and how light it was to hold. He stroked the wood and iron for a long time, and read Byron the engraving: *Samuel Colt, Paterson, New Jersey.*

"I'm headin' west," said Josh. "I wanna head for the Mississippi and just keep on goin', 'cause I'm tired of Illinois."

Byron made no reply. Josh cocked the hammer, uncocked it again, and put the revolver in his belt.

He set off with the men behind him and Lord Byron at his side, an invisible companion. Joshua loved him very much. Only occasionally did a slight displeasure creep over him, because there was one thing about his friend that bothered him: his incessant, pig-headed rhyming. Byron sometimes almost reminded him of his father when he was drunk and sang "Barbara Allan."

They reached the Mississippi at the mouth of the Fox River, where they encountered a group of Englishmen who were coming upstream to enjoy the countryside, scout for Indians, and prepare sketches for an account of their journey. They had left the landing stage and were riding inland with an armed guide. The gentlemen returned safe and sound to the Mississippi, albeit without money, without watches, and without an escort too. They refrained from remarking upon Joshua's ancestors because the British are polite, and in any case they had no eye for such things. They were expecting Indian braves with bows and arrows, their faces painted and their heads crowned with feathers, and not a boy with a revolver. They said nothing, turned their pockets out, and survived the outing unscathed. They even received a "thank you," because Josh found a book.

He made camp for the night. He ate with the men and ordered one of them to keep watch. Then he looked to see what he had acquired. It was a slender volume in black leather: Douglas Fortescue, *Colors*. They were poems, or perhaps just a single one. It was hard to say. It went on so, page after page, words, broken sentences, and there wasn't a single rhyme. Joshua read *Colors* from cover to cover, unable to move, a piece of rock in the grass. He hardly noticed that the fire was almost scorching his sleeve. When he had finished reading *Colors*, he started again from the beginning.

A swamp, a river
A muddy brown like coffee
Eating the colors away.
And there are roses, or snakes,
Slithering flowers
Half drowned in languid waters.

Joshua shook his head. Then he unrolled his blanket and lay
down to sleep. He took the book with him under the blanket.
It was light and slender like Mr Colt's gun.

Joshua Jenkyns set out with Fortescue in his coat pocket.
Slithering flowers. He didn't know what that was supposed
to mean. He looked around him. He even dismounted and
studied a couple of flowers, dog tooth violet and prairie
smoke. They weren't slithering anywhere. Joshua crossed
the Mississippi. He was jumpy. He caused a bloodbath in
Dubuque. One of his men was shot, so Josh rubbed gunpowder into the wound and set light to it, a trick Father had used
to prevent putrefaction. *Roses or snakes.* Joshua wasn't sure
whether he liked this Fortescue. He slept badly and dreamt
nonsense. They were watering the horses at the Red Cedar
River when he dropped his loading rod into the water. They
rode on towards Muscatine. One morning Joshua noticed that
Byron had gone, and another rode in his place: Fortescue.
Joshua realized he liked him after all. Eventually he asked him
if he wanted to go westward too, and Fortescue once again

talked about muddy brown rivers. Joshua mulled it over. Then he said, "Hmm." The men had known for a long time that he spoke with ghosts, but they made no comment. You didn't talk to Josh. He hated that. And of course there was nothing whatsoever to say in any case.

Joshua turned around and rode westward for days and weeks on end. He wouldn't have dared to make this journey with Byron. Now he dared to make it with Fortescue. Joshua was afraid of this journey. He was afraid of Indians.

He read *Colors* every day. He whispered it to himself. He occasionally shouted the strange words into the air: Joshua's talismans. Then he saw them, Ioways and Mesquakies, a couple of families on the move. Josh gritted his teeth and drove his horse forward. The reins grew damp in his hand. The Indians had skinny ponies, skinny women and children, hides, and folded tents. They let him pass unmolested, and then they were gone. Joshua spat. He was terrified of Indians. What were you supposed to do with them? Because Joshua had a secret: he wasn't allowed to shoot at Indians.

He'd known this ever since he'd been able to think. You were allowed to shoot at anyone, even at your own men if they became insolent, and if need be at women and children who got in the way—Josh was allowed to shoot at anyone, but not at Indians. He didn't know why. Nobody had taught him this rule. It was simply there, and Josh was obliged to respect it. Don't shoot at redskins. And what are you supposed to do with someone you can't or mustn't or don't want to shoot at? Wave? Talk maybe? One of those hand signals that mean "friend" or "peace" or "barter"? Father had drummed these signs into Josh, but he sure as hell wouldn't use them.

He encountered other Indians on the long journey. Sometimes their paths crossed so close that he could smell their hides, still fresh and bloody. The Indians were peaceful. Once they almost greeted him. Josh shuddered. Didn't the Indians want to shoot at Joshua Jenkyns either? Maybe that was even worse. But Fortescue comforted him, and each time it chased the Indians away. And it was hardly a surprise to Joshua when he arrived at the river, the mighty brown waters that oozed sluggishly over mud and trees that had been burst asunder. Joshua had long since canonized the poet. Of course Fortescue knew it. *A swamp, a river, a muddy brown like coffee*—Josh dismounted and dug a hole by the bank wherein he hastily and unceremoniously buried his Byron.

Young Josh Jenkyns henceforth remained faithful to two gods: the poet and the river, Fortescue and the Missouri.

$\mathcal{V}$

I N THE SPRING OF 1841, Douglas Fortescue put aside his pen and thereafter described himself as having retired. He was weary of the tittle-tattle. For a few months now, he had been absorbed by a new pastime: photography. It had been love at first sight, long before he actually held a plate in his hands. All it had required was a brief article in *Fashionable Life* about Monsieur Daguerre's invention. Using light to capture the living world on silver-coated copper—Douglas knew straight away that a device capable of this should be his weapon of choice.

As for being famous, he had planned it, made it a reality, and perhaps enjoyed it too, but now it lay behind him. He had earned enough money. No more books appeared after *The Waltz,* and gone were the days when a poet issued invitations to dancing and chloroform in the white palace by Regent's

Park. Douglas bought his first camera, and moved to the green fields of Greenwich.

Jeremy could scarcely believe his luck. He happily turned his back on London, and even though he couldn't understand what use it was, he willingly lent his brother a hand. Together they unraveled the secrets of the photographic apparatus. Together they opened the shutter for the first time. For twelve long minutes the three of them stared at a tree in the sunshine: Douglas, Jeremy, and the camera. Then the image was captured, and the mercury vapor revealed it to the eye: the faint ghost of a tree. "Salvation," said Douglas. "From what?" asked Jeremy. "From *la dolce vita*, which is constantly moving too fast," said Douglas with a smile. Henceforth Jeremy Fortescue avoided such questions.

Douglas wasn't satisfied with trees. He made swift progress, and soon acquired his second camera. A meniscus lens considerably improved matters. He now took pictures of people. A picture of Jeremy. A picture of his disconcerted neighbors. Pictures of random passers-by. Pictures of Jeremy's children, visiting from Harrow and Yorkshire. Douglas immobilized them all in velvet-upholstered clamps, no matter who they were; at least they were people. His happiness depended on the exposure time. In the late spring of 1841 he managed his first picture under thirty-five seconds.

London took umbrage at the poet's desertion. The publishers missed his books and society was robbed of a much-loved attraction. The photographer did not receive visitors in Greenwich. The *beau monde* was far too fidgety for his clamps. Fatal Fortescue soon became nothing but a memory, although many recollections remained hazy. A young man called Donnie was distraught to find that he recalled a muddy brown river and all manner of peculiar things besides. He consulted Lord Warrington's son. Lord Warrington's son also recalled some shady doings. Who had composed Fortescue's poems? And what did Fatal Fortescue do late at night? The youth named Donnie ran to his father. The father ran to Lord Warrington. Lord Warrington consulted Douglas' publisher, and then Scotland Yard too.

In June 1841 they charged Douglas Fortescue with deception, and in July with sodomy. "A-ha," said Douglas. He carefully rotated a silvery plate in the iodine vapor. Jeremy asked and asked. "Deception, yes," said Douglas when he could no longer bear the interrogation. "Sodomy, no. How strange. What is it?"

Jeremy was disinclined to wait for the trials. He advocated flight. He rejected Paris, Vienna, and St Petersburg. Speed was of the essence. Douglas repeatedly photographed a child with a sheep on the meadow adjoining the house. The pictures were blurred. Douglas asked Jeremy to build a frame in which he could clamp the child and the sheep.

"America," said Jeremy.

"Just put a clamp on that damned ball of wool," countered

Douglas gently, "otherwise I'm afraid I shall have to cut its throat."

Jeremy Fortescue ordered an all-metal miniature camera with an achromatic lens from Herr Steinheil in Munich. Then he booked the passage from Liverpool to New Orleans.

"What?" asked Douglas. "America?"

Jeremy began to explain. He wanted to buy land, lots of land; it could be had cheaply there. He wanted to cultivate the land. He wanted to start afresh. He wanted to send for the children if everything went well. He wanted a brother, blond and well-nourished, under the sun of Illinois. "Like honest people," said Jeremy. He said that several times. When he repeated it for the fourth time, Douglas gently reminded him whose money he was planning to spend in the New World. The color drained from Jeremy's face. Douglas smiled. "Come now, darling," he said, "I'd accompany you to the North Pole if you promised me the light was good there."

"The light is good," sighed Jeremy.

"And nobody reads poetry, do they?"

"No," said Jeremy, "I'm certain that nobody in Illinois reads poetry."

The Steinheil camera looked strange: Douglas thought it was a cross between a gun and an enema syringe. Nevertheless, it enabled an exposure time of just fourteen seconds, so he rapidly forgave its ludicrous shape. He took photographs in Liverpool, of women laborers standing in front of chimneys.

He took photographs at sea, of a harpooned dolphin and the ship's mate on the bowsprit: sharp, good contrasts, entirely without clamps. He took photographs on the Mississippi. He took photographs in New Orleans. He had no luck with alligators, but was most astonished to discover that Negroes and magnolias proved to be a great success. "A delightful trip," said Douglas. "Thank you, Jeremy *chéri*." And then he took a photograph of a barber in the Rue Burgundy, and got him to touch up his roots.

The Fortescue brothers spent the winter in New Orleans, and then embarked on a steamer that sailed up the Mississippi to Memphis. Douglas took photographs of the passengers, of Jeremy, who was bent over the real estate advertisements with his pencil at the ready, and of the cotton that came toward them, still grainy and impure, grayish-brown clouds which the boats could barely contain. "What a charming nightmare," said Douglas, and opened the aperture.

From Memphis they carried on to St Louis, where they took up residence. Douglas shot family portraits for the fur barons, proudly assembled in front of their Greek villas built of Missouri granite, frozen in time like a still life. Then he pursued the whores and hoodlums down by the river. An old man in a Cossack tunic sheepishly removed his hat for the Englishman, and was rewarded with a photograph of his scalped head. Douglas had long since been giving the plates away. He derived no pleasure from collecting them. Douglas

Fortescue took aim at the fleeting moment, which had barely been captured before he consigned it to oblivion.

Jeremy had found his land, which belonged to the state. You had to go to Fayette County to be entered on the register. Jeremy showed Douglas the map. "Silver iodide," Douglas muttered. Jeremy booked seats in the stagecoach, and he took cash with him to pay for the land. He also left money and some of the luggage in St Louis. "I see," said Douglas. "Illinois! I believe you did mention it once."

On 10 April 1842 the Fortescues set off for Vandalia, heading north from St Louis because they had to follow the road. They drove four-in-hand, with three riders providing the escort. The camera sat on Douglas's knees since the roof didn't seem safe to him. Coated plates awaited in a case that protected them from the sun. You never knew what you might come across on your journey: beautiful scenery, good light.

They shared the coach with a family: a man, two women, and a child. They answered to the name of Stalmaker. The father was called Augustus, the mother Priscilla, and the little son Abinadi. The second woman named Phebe was still expecting her child, of whom Mr Stalmaker was also the father. The Fortescues learned all this when they had scarcely left St Louis behind them. Stalmaker was a talkative fellow. He claimed that all the Stalmakers were saints, and latter-day ones at that. They were bound for Nauvoo to baptize their late ancestors, and would then head westward into the Promised

Land. Amulek was the name of the unborn child, because its father said it would be a boy. This was the will of God and that of the prophet Joseph Smith.

The road was bad. Abinadi cried, and Phebe vomited out of the window. Jeremy groaned, while Douglas said nothing. He laid a thin white cloth over his face since he didn't care for the dust and was concerned about his complexion. Thus veiled, he sat and silently endured what Mr Stalmaker and the Book of Mormon had to say to him. He took a photograph of the holy family. He endured the wretched overnight accommodation without demur. Next morning he shaved, applied oil to his hair, brushed his black velvet frock coat, and then enveloped his face again and took his seat in the coach. He scarcely felt the jolts from the road. Douglas Fortescue sat motionless, his face covered, the camera on his lap.

"Rise up," intoned Mr Stalmaker solemnly, "and pass this Jordan, thee and all thy people, to the land which I have given to the children of Israel."

VI

HALF A DAY'S JOURNEY BEFORE Carrolton, the coach suddenly jolted to a standstill. Douglas reached for his camera. He heard a shout, and then a shot. The women screamed. Stalmaker began to pray out loud. Then there was another bang, then one more, and then a fourth. Something heavy crashed to the ground. Something hit the roof of the coach. "God almighty," cried Jeremy. One final shot, and then it was all over.

The travelers sat speechless. Priscilla held Abinadi's mouth tight shut. Nobody dared to open the blinds. Douglas exhaled a faint "Oh" without unveiling his face. Somebody tore open the door: he had a red beard and hair, was unkempt and covered in dust, and his teeth were blackened. "Men outside," he ordered, and dragged Jeremy and Mr Stalmaker from the carriage. Douglas was sitting next to Priscilla and Phebe, facing the direction of travel. He didn't stir. He was unwilling to feel that this order applied to him, and the bandit doubtless thought he was a lady too, since he left the veiled man in peace. Douglas gingerly bent forward and carefully observed the scene. The material covering his eyes was thin enough.

The red-haired man placed Jeremy and Stalmaker with their faces against the coach, their hands raised and their legs apart. A similar pose was adopted by the driver and two of the riders, one of whom had a bloody hand. Their weapons were neatly gathered at the side of the road. The third man who had formed part of the escort lay prostrate on the road while his horse nibbled leaves from a bush. The red Devil had two sidekicks, one blond and the other gray, all of them old rather than young. They searched the travelers for weapons. They found a pepperbox revolver on Stalmaker, and nothing on Jeremy.

"Undress," ordered the redhead. Stalmaker prayed. Jeremy gritted his teeth. Douglas looked at the man on the road. He was lying peacefully, his face in the dust and his knees together. One of the bandits climbed over him and reached for Mr Stalmaker.

The saint cried out. The bandit hit him. The saint silently slipped out of his coat. Jeremy nervously copied him, becoming entangled in a sleeve. He was standing just in front of the open door, close to his brother. Douglas could see the horror in his eyes. Jeremy could see nothing but a white cloth.

They had to strip to their undergarments. The bandits knew where people hid their money. Douglas watched them take his brother's purse, English gold to buy his land. Stalmaker had silver. The man with the red beard took a long knife and cut it from the lining of his waistcoat, a task he was evidently used to performing. Douglas bent a little further forward and could now see the fourth man. He was sitting quietly on his horse, a rifle in front of him and a small handgun in his right hand. The barrel was lowered, pointing at the pommel on his saddle. The horse, a graceful pinto, kept as still as its rider. The sun was shining brightly on this frozen image. The rider was beardless and bareheaded. He had knotted a twisted bandana around his tousled black curls, which were covered in dust as if they had been powdered. He was very young. He kept a straight face. He seemed to be overseeing the proceedings.

Douglas noticed that this rider was distracting his attention from Jeremy, who stood in front of the coach in his sweaty underwear, defenseless and affronted. Douglas stared past him, and slowly raised the veil. He scrutinized the rider as if he were a painting in a gallery. Sun. Shadow. A pinto and a boy made of stone, dressed like a cattle drover, rustic and unwashed. It was only when he felt the metal in his fingers that Douglas realized what he was doing. He had taken a plate from the case and was adjusting the lens.

Jeremy hadn't taken his eyes off his brother whilst being forced to undress in front of two women, between a fresh corpse and a whining bigamist. Jeremy caught his breath. Douglas was fiddling with his camera as if it were Mardi

Gras in New Orleans. He was lovingly tinkering with his lens, scarcely three feet away from a man who'd been shot. "Douglas, stop it," whispered Jeremy. Douglas seemed not to hear him. He was fumbling with the screws that held the lens. Jeremy wanted to whisper one more time. He shouted instead.

"Are you out of your mind, Douglas Fortescue?" roared Jeremy, and he roared so loud that Douglas dropped his plate.

A shot. Priscilla whimpered. It was the boy who had fired, a shot into the dust. He pulled a face that Douglas couldn't interpret. The man with the red beard hit Jeremy in the face. The boy dismounted. He aimed his gun at Jeremy. Jeremy had crashed into the coach, and he stood swaying, his nose bleeding. The rider slowly walked up to him, rather stiffly, as if he'd been riding for a very long time. He cast a very brief glance into the coach, at Douglas and the women. Then he cleared his throat. "Mister," asked the boy, "what did you just shout out?"

Jeremy didn't reply. The boy raised his gun. He was shorter than Jeremy, and thinner too. The toe of his boot was touching the dead man.

"I said, 'Douglas Fortescue, are you out of your mind?'" hissed Jeremy.

"What?"

"'Douglas Fortescue, are you out of your mind!'"

"Where?" asked the boy.

"That's me," said Douglas. "I'm Douglas Fortescue: Englishman, writer, unarmed. Please don't shoot us."

The boy pushed Jeremy aside and now stood in front of the door.

"Fortescue," he said in a flat voice.

"Yes, I'm afraid so," countered Douglas.

"Fortescue," repeated the boy, as if it were a magic spell or perhaps a swearword. He briefly looked Douglas in the face, blinked, and lowered his gaze. The barrel of his gun was pointing at the bottom of Douglas's nose. Douglas looked into the muzzle, and so it remained for a long while. The silence was unbearable. The only sound was of Abinadi sobbing, half suffocated in Priscilla's maternal grasp.

Suddenly the boy stepped back and issued his orders. "Get that man out!" Redbeard dragged Douglas from the coach. "Guns." Redbeard shoved Douglas against the coach, searched him, and found nothing. "Take him over to my horse." Redbeard cast a questioning look at the boy. "Take him over," repeated the boy menacingly. The redhead obeyed.

Douglas offered no resistance. The boy indicated the pinto. Douglas asked: "Me?" The boy nodded, and held the stirrup for Douglas. And Douglas Fortescue clambered into the saddle, clumsily, his cloth still covering his well-oiled long black hair.

Jeremy took a while to understand. They were taking his brother away from him, and he was powerless to do anything

49

about it. "I've got money in St Louis," he shouted. "Please gen-tlemen! English pounds!" Nobody paid any attention to him. The boy tied Douglas's hands to the pommel. Douglas was staring all the while at Jeremy, a look of reproach on his face.

The boy mounted the dead man's horse. He took the reins of the pinto, knee to knee with the hostage. "Why?" whispered Douglas. The boy didn't spare him a glance. The bandits had unsaddled the horses belonging to the remaining escorts and then tied them together, intending to take them with them.

"I'd like my camera," whispered Douglas. He didn't get the camera. He cast a final glance at Jeremy, who was be-wildered, disgusted, and dumbfounded. And so it was that Jeremy Fortescue stood on a dusty road in Illinois, without money, without trousers, but with a swollen nose, watching helplessly as his brother was being led off. It was beyond him. Why Douglas? What did they want with Douglas Fortescue? There he rode, his back stiff, his legs awkwardly spread apart. A half-grown savage was holding his reins, and Douglas still had this veil over his hair, like a young bride. They were rid-ing at right angles to the road, heading northwest across open country. Jeremy watched them go.

"The Lord punishes his children," intoned Stalmaker sol-emnly, whereupon Jeremy slapped him in the face. Then he burst into tears.

VII

D OUGLAS SAW A FARM, and then nothing more. This was Jeremy's virgin territory. They rode for a good hour at a leisurely pace, a quiet procession. It was sunny and windless. There was grass, but that was all, grass stretching to the horizon. Douglas would gladly have gotten rid of the cloth that was hanging into his eyes, but his hands weren't free. Everything hurt. Douglas hadn't ridden since leaving Yorkshire, since he felt that the back of a horse was decidedly no place for a poet.

The boy rode in silence, his head lowered. Douglas discreetly located his weapons. He had placed the rifle through two leather loops on his saddle, and the handgun in his belt. It was a small pistol with a cylinder between the handle and the barrel.

Suddenly the boy began to shout, with no prior warning or visible cause. At first it seemed as if he was trying to form a word, but then it was just a noise, a clear, loud cry across the grassland, a cry of joy, a cry for help, a cry of horror or exuberance—Douglas was unable to figure it out. When he was done with shouting, he exhaled a kind of sigh and wound Douglas's reins even tighter around his hand.

The grass reached over the stirrups. Douglas was light-headed. He'd had no breakfast, having relied as always on the shortbread that Jeremy kept in his carpetbag. There was no shortbread here, no Jeremy, and no camera either.

The boy ordered a rest. He untied Douglas. Douglas looked at his knuckles, which had been rubbed raw by the rope. The boy looked at them too, then offered Douglas his hand and helped him dismount. He gave him a leather bottle from which he drank some water.

"What is the meaning of all this?" asked Douglas. The boy made no reply.

"What do you want from me?" Silence. The three men were laboriously counting the loot, coin by coin. They said a number to the boy. He nodded. Then he took the veil from Douglas's head, tore it up, and made it into two bandages for his wrists.

"Do you have a name?" asked Douglas, much to his own surprise. He spoke like a schoolmaster. His kidnapper cleared his throat, staring at his boots in the grass. Then he reached for his gun.

"Pardon me," said Douglas.

The boy cleared his throat once more. "Joshua," he muttered, almost incomprehensible. Then he pushed Douglas towards the horse and held the stirrup for him again. He also retied the rope firmly over his bandaged wrists.

They rode until dusk, until they reached a spot where the grass wasn't all that high, where there was wood and a little water, an almost dried-up stream, with a couple of rocks. This was where the riders would spend the night. Douglas sat on a stone. He felt dizzy. He watched Joshua's men as they unsaddled the horses, led them to the water, and then hobbled them for the night. Then they gathered wood and made a fire. The sun set. The sky was red. It was picturesque yet absurd. Joshua crouched in the grass and cleaned his weapons.

The gray-haired man roasted something over the fire. Douglas gagged when he smelled it. He scanned the surrounding countryside, Jeremy's damned America. Douglas screwed his mouth into something resembling a grin. What would Jeremy be doing? Douglas grinned, gagged, and grinned again. He wondered whether he was afraid. He didn't know. He didn't feel too good.

When his men announced that dinner was ready, Joshua invited the poet to come to the fire. Douglas already understood the wordless commands. He received his share, a large piece of whatever smelled so ghastly. He shook his head. Joshua made a noise that sounded like "hmm." "No thank you," said Douglas, "I don't want any." The roast meat not only smelled bad, but was very greasy too. Douglas didn't eat greasy food. Douglas never ate greasy food. Even the barren prairie wouldn't succeed in converting Douglas Fortescue to greasy food.

Joshua frowned and then drew his revolver.

"Oh God," said Douglas. He ate the greasy substance, accompanied by rather too much of something hard that was made of flour. "Hmm," said Joshua whenever Douglas grimaced. He dutifully ate. Indeed, he ate his most substantial meal in fifteen years, by this fire in the middle of nowhere. He was overjoyed when Joshua decided he had eaten enough, and managed to suppress one final gag. Only now did Joshua permit himself to eat.

Douglas wiped his mouth and glanced at the men. Large, stupid faces. They had eaten their fill. Two of them unrolled their blankets and lay down to sleep. The blond grabbed his rifle and took up his position.

"Do they have names too?" asked Douglas.

Joshua nodded.

"And what might they be?"

Joshua chewed, swallowed, cleared his throat, and then raised his hand.

"Absolum," said Joshua, pointing to the lookout.

"Zadock." He indicated the man with the red beard, who was already snoring.

"And Paradise," said Joshua. This was the grizzled cook.

Douglas began to laugh. He couldn't stop himself. He felt much better. The greasy stuff had agreed remarkably well with him, and now he laughed out of desperation, exhaustion, and helplessness.

Joshua suddenly looked into his face. He blinked, but stood his ground. Douglas fell silent. He stared back. He stared into the boy's black eyes.

"Forgive me," said Douglas, "but those names ..."

Joshua fought hard. He wanted to turn away, but didn't. He stared at Douglas, frowning and with his lips pressed tight shut.

"Joshua ..." began Douglas. Joshua winced. He already had his hand on his revolver again. Was it forbidden to call him by this name?

"Joshua," repeated Douglas defiantly. Joshua cleared his throat and spat into the fire.

Douglas was given a blanket and the pinto's saddle as a pillow. He had to lie down and cover himself. Joshua sat next to him, deftly casting bullets and then filing the burrs. Douglas lay motionless, replete, and watched him. Once he'd finished his bullets, Joshua caught lice. He did so with the same calm and circumspection. He flicked the lice into the embers. Then he retied the bandana around his head, fetched a blanket and lay down, almost shoulder to shoulder with Douglas. The person named Zadock snored and wheezed. Douglas reached for the saddle. He wanted to move away from his kidnapper. He didn't smell good. He had lice. Joshua shook his head. Douglas stayed where he was.

"And just where would I go if I ran away?" asked Douglas after a long silence. He didn't expect a reply.

Joshua wasn't asleep. He was staring at the sky. Douglas studied his profile, black against the glowing embers. A straight forehead, a soft chin, a gently curved nose. Douglas didn't want to sleep either. He realized he was frightened after all.

Douglas Fortescue and Joshua Jenkyns were frightened all night long, and they were glad when morning came. There was a kind of coffee with bacon and dough cakes, a hearty breakfast for the poet. Joshua cocked his revolver. Douglas sighed and ate.

"Tie your hair back, mister; it'll just get in the way," murmured Joshua, and handed Douglas a piece of cord. Douglas obeyed. "Thank you," he said, "that's a good idea."

Joshua examined Douglas's wrists. They were still raw, despite the bandages. Joshua thought for a long time. Then he pushed his untied captive towards the horse. "A-ha," said Douglas. Joshua snarled at him, fierce, a disagreeable sound. Douglas nodded. He certainly wouldn't get any silly ideas with his freed hands. He pulled a face and mounted, even before Joshua grabbed the stirrup. It was very straightforward. Douglas dispassionately realized that one never forgets how to ride. He wasn't given the reins. He casually held on to the pommel, and Joshua led him westward, followed by Absolum, Zadock, and Paradise.

They rode into a town called Pleasance: a street, a couple of houses, a sheriff, a gallows. They needed flour and gunpowder and boots for Fortescue; he could no longer ride in these shoes. The street in Pleasance emptied, and the sheriff took refuge in his jail. Absolum and Zadock stopped off for some liquor, there were a couple of shots, but nobody came to any harm. Paradise made the purchases. There was no cobbler in Pleasance. Joshua knew that sheriffs often had good boots, so after a moment's hesitation he shoved Douglas into the jail. The sheriff fired indiscriminately with a scatter of gunshot. He missed both Josh and his hostage. Joshua quickly disarmed him, then placed him in front of Douglas and pointed the barrel of his revolver at his boots.

"That's fine by me," said Douglas, "but let him live."

Henceforth the poet rode in the sheriff of Pleasance's boots. Paradise launched into a song. It sounded bad, and after the first verse Josh ordered him to hold his tongue. He would have liked to shout, but he knew that didn't help. He clenched his teeth. It was a difficult journey.

Fortescue now had boots, but his reins were still in Joshua's hand. Fortescue had blond stubble and black hair, which puzzled Josh. He ate twice a day; Josh made sure of that. He stayed because Josh kept hold of him. Nevertheless, it was a difficult journey for Joshua Jenkyns. Fortescue, the prophet of the Missouri, had gone. Instead of him, this man was riding at his side. Joshua couldn't talk to him. He wondered whether he should shoot him, but he didn't have the heart to do so.

Douglas was also at a loss. What did the boy want from him? Why did he steal boots for him? Why the deuce was he fattening him up? A ransom hadn't been mentioned. Joshua gave no reply to Douglas's questions, although he eventually got used to his own name. Douglas often said it, for no reason whatsoever: "Joshua." The saddlebags of the pinto that he'd now been riding for so long contained five books: *Thirst, Pain, Dreams, The Waltz,* and *Colors.* Joshua had gone to great lengths to acquire them. Douglas didn't know that. Joshua didn't tell him either. He swallowed and spat and cleared his throat, but words defeated him.

Joshua's men couldn't understand what all this meant either. Why was this stranger given this horse? That was utterly unfathomable for Absolum, Zadock, and Paradise. Josh would never have lent the pinto, so why had he given it to the hostage? Absolum, Zadock, and Paradise secretly tried to discuss this by the fire, turned away from Douglas and Josh. They groaned. Talking hurt. They failed to reach any conclusion.

VIII

J EREMY RODE AT FULL GALLOP to Carrolton on a coach
horse. He found the sheriff and yelled at him.

"I see," said the sheriff when he finally understood.
"An ambush! I sure am sorry to hear that sir."

Jeremy told him about the hostage-taking, and described
the bandits.

"And why did they kidnap your brother?" enquired the
sheriff.

"I don't know," cried Jeremy. "I want him back!"

He was forced to describe the bandits again. The sheriff
smiled, almost a little misty-eyed. "Little Josh," he said. Then
he thought for a long while. He went through the story, and
then realized the Englishman was lying.

"Josh Jenkyns don't take no hostages," he said severely.
"Don't pull my leg."

Jeremy bought a horse and rode back to St Louis. Joshua

had made a bad job of the robbery, and had left a great deal behind. There had still been gold and silver in the coach: Jeremy's gold and Stalmaker's silver. It was enough for a horse. It was also enough for the journey to Nauvoo. Abinadi's diaper almost contained more than Mr Stalmaker's waistcoat, and the saints duly continued their journey.

The Stalmakers brought a peculiar treasure to Nauvoo. The Prophet Joseph Smith couldn't make head or tail of it. At first glance he thought the thing was a mighty odd pistol. He shut himself into the temple and gave it a thorough examination. A wooden handle, a fat barrel made of metal, a lens, and a box of plates into the bargain. The Prophet removed the plates. They were silver, but then they turned black. That was mysterious. He looked at the plates, but they withheld their secrets. They were black now, and they didn't get any blacker. He prayed, but nothing happened. And so Joseph Smith built a shrine and buried the apparatus together with the black plates next to the font for the dead. He said a blessing over it and kept the matter to himself.

Douglas Fortescue no longer had a camera. He didn't even have smoked-glass spectacles. For good or ill, he was obliged to look through his own green eyes. He saw grass and sky, horses, a boy, three men, and the moon, the stars, and the fire at night. He lost any sense of time. Every day he expected

to fall dead from his horse: Fatal Fortescue, the fragile ghost
of the salons. But he didn't fall from his horse, which he occasionally regretted. His hair became matted and his black
velvet coat was gray from the dust.

Douglas desperately wanted a shave. On the third day of his
captivity he asked Joshua for his knife, and tried his luck with
it. The lack of soap made things difficult. He cut himself, but
then somehow it worked: his cheeks, yes, but not his chest.
One doesn't do that with a strange knife, thought Douglas.
He wiped it and handed it back to Joshua, who stared at it as
if he'd never seen it before.

On the morning of the eighth day they reached the Mississippi, where they found a ferry and crossed to the other side.
They paid like honest folk. Stalmaker's coins gave Joshua an
idea. On the other bank he took Jeremy's purse, the gold for
buying his land, and pressed it into Douglas's hand.

"What am I supposed to do with that?" asked Douglas.

Joshua made no reply. Absolum simply uttered, "Oh."
Joshua threw him a glance, which promptly silenced him.
Douglas held the gold, overcome with confusion.

"Why are you giving me that, Joshua?"

Joshua said nothing. The men mounted their horses.

"Joshua ..." Douglas was surprised by his own voice. Maybe
it was down to this name, which sounded like a term of en-
dearment, but maybe not. Joshua fingered his gun.

"If I were to ask you," enquired Douglas quietly, since he

didn't want the men to hear, "if I were to ask you very sincerely, would you let me go?"

Joshua shook his head. Douglas put Jeremy's gold away. He didn't ask this question again.

They rode on to a place where the Mississippi had lost its outlines, where there were pools and a great many mosquitoes. Absolum, Zadock, and Paradise had to keep guard because Joshua went for a swim. He reluctantly handed Zadock his revolver, with a fierce stare. Then he undressed and jumped into the water while the men stood on the bank, their rifles resting vigilantly in the crooks of their arms.

Douglas watched Joshua swimming. He swam and dived; maybe he was trying to drown his lice. He soon got out again, and immediately reached for his gun. Douglas had to smile, since the naked boy with the revolver was an amusing sight. Joshua squatted on a stone and began to wash his clothes. Not one single drop touched the gun.

"I should like to bathe too," said Douglas.

Joshua shook his head.

"Might I wash my clothes?"

Joshua hesitated, and then nodded.

Douglas removed his coat, waistcoat, and shirt. He glanced at his chest. Pale blond stubble. Douglas groaned. If it carried on like this, they would start to curl. He reached for the fly of his trousers, but then paused and decided to keep them on.

"If only you knew what you were doing to me," sighed Douglas, and laid his shirt in the water. They crouched peacefully next to one another. Douglas rubbed the shirt, and then he saw from Joshua that one had to beat the washing against the stone, so he copied him. They shared the water of the Mississippi as it lapped the bank, and they shared the mosquitoes too.

Douglas spread his shirt to dry, then sat down again. Joshua was still washing. He was crouching down, his heels in the air and his knees under his armpits. Douglas wondered why he didn't fall over. Joshua had long toes which he was probably using to hold on to the stone, like a parrot on its perch. Douglas leaned back slightly. The revolver lay to the right beside Joshua, while Douglas sat to the left. The horses were grazing nearby, and the men were off in the distance, shooting at ducks. Douglas looked at Joshua's toes, his brown legs, and his shoulder blades which stood out under his skin. His hair fell into his face. He was vigorously slapping his wet headband onto the stone. Douglas held his breath for a moment. Run. Now. A well-placed blow, a grab for the revolver, ten paces to the horse, and then up and away. Douglas leaned even slightly further back. The revolver. He knew it was loaded, but he didn't know whether he'd be able to cock it right away. A push, the revolver in the water ... and then? Douglas was wearing trousers and boots. Joshua was barefoot and naked. Douglas slowly breathed out. It was twenty years since his last fight, a blond country lad in Yorkshire ... Would he? Could he? How would it turn out? Joshua, naked and angry: how quickly would he be on his feet? How soon would he reach Douglas? How hard would it be to hold him, to bring him to the ground?

"No way, mister," said Joshua Jenkyns.

There was duck that evening. Douglas ate of his own accord. He would fast later on, once he had survived his current dilemma; now he had to eat, otherwise Joshua aimed his gun at him, and Douglas didn't like gazing into its black muzzle. He would put on weight and look like a farmer, and Jeremy wouldn't recognize him if he turned up. Jeremy? But of course, thought Douglas, he's bound to turn up. Jeremy always comes when you need him. He gnawed assiduously at a bone.

Joshua posted two lookouts that night, because it was a vulnerable location. Paradise was allowed to sleep. Joshua shooed him away from the fire, away from the hostage. He gave Douglas his saddle and blanket and lay next to him, as close as ever.

"No bullets today?" asked Douglas.

Joshua shook his head.

"And the lice have been drowned?"

Joshua closed his eyes. He lay on his back in a deathlike pose, the revolver by his side. He was breathing quietly. He was asleep.

Douglas waited for a long time. Then he stretched out his hand, slowly and deliberately, and laid it on the revolver.

Joshua wasn't asleep. He grabbed Douglas's hand, grasped his gun firmly, and hissed.

"What a work of art," said Douglas. "I've never seen anything like it."

Joshua sat up and bared his teeth. He reached for Douglas's shoulder and immediately let it go again.

"It has a cylinder, doesn't it?" Douglas smiled. "Will you show it to me?"

Joshua chewed his bottom lip. Suddenly he emptied the cylinder and held the revolver out for Douglas. With the other hand he reached for his rifle.

"A-ha," said Douglas. He turned the slender weapon in his hands, moved the cylinder, examined the loading rod, studied the trigger mechanism that reacted to the movement of the hammer.

"Beautiful," said Douglas. "What is it called?"

He returned the revolver to Joshua. Joshua loaded it: powder, five plugs, five bullets. Joshua bent down toward the fire and gently stroked two fingers over the lock. Then he said quietly: "Samuel Colt, Paterson, New Jersey. It's written on there. It shoots good."

"I believe you," answered Douglas. He looked at the engraving himself.

"I can read," murmured Joshua. He sounded amazed, almost anxious.

Douglas nodded. He slowly lifted his hand and came closer. He could feel Joshua's breath. Douglas moved his hand, slowly, slowly, slowly. Joshua swallowed. Douglas's hand was next to his, touching the loaded revolver. Douglas closed his fingers around it. Joshua swallowed again. Douglas slowly took the gun from his hand, held it by the barrel, and carefully turned it round. He examined all of it again: the engraving, the cylinder, the lock. He looked up. Joshua stared into his eyes, unable to move. Douglas cocked the hammer and smiled. He aimed at the embers, and uncocked it again. Then he took Joshua's hand, laid the revolver in it, and closed Joshua's fingers around it.

"Thank you," said Douglas. "That's a handsome invention."

He lay down, adjusted the saddle, turned his back on Joshua, and pulled the blanket over his head.

That night, Joshua Jenkyns realized that things were getting dangerous. Something had to happen. He pointed the gun at Douglas's back, let if fall, and aimed again. He did so several times. Eventually he gave up. Joshua would have to speak, but he didn't know how to. He thought about it, hour after hour. He couldn't find a sentence to say to Fortescue, no word, no explanation, nothing whatsoever. In the middle of the night he got up and fetched *Colors*. It was still his favorite book. He held *Colors* without opening it; he knew it by heart. He sat with *Colors* next to the dying embers. He would have liked to shout, but he didn't want to wake Fortescue. He returned *Colors* to the other books and continued to chew things over. He came up with things to say, rejected them, and then came up with new ones. He suddenly found a great many of them. Josh Jenkyns had enough sentences to choose from when morning finally came. He just had to decide.

When Douglas awoke, he found himself staring into the muzzle of the revolver. Joshua was looking calmly into his face, with his lips relaxed. What beautiful lips he had if only he didn't press them together: full, dark, sharply outlined lips.

He casually aimed between Douglas's eyes. "I love you, mister," said Joshua. This was the sentence he liked best.

IX

JOSH JENKYNS LEFT IT at that. He breakfasted with a
hearty appetite, and soon shooed Douglas onto his horse.
Joshua whistled up his men. "Fort Howard," he said,
curling his lips until they almost formed a grin. Then he
grabbed Douglas's reins and they set off.

Douglas scratched distractedly at his mosquito bites. Why
was Joshua in such a good mood now? He mulled over Joshua's
meager disclosure: those four grotesque words. Nobody had
ever uttered such nonsense to Douglas Fortescue. The boy
was unhinged. He was mistaking him for someone else. But
for whom? Douglas groaned, and wondered whether anyone
could mistake him for someone who would deserve such a
sentence. Unlikely, he thought. He remembered Joshua's gun
in his hand, loaded and cocked. He pondered this at great
length too, but to no avail.

At noon they reached a hill above the settlement that Joshua called Fort Howard: squat houses, lots of wood and not much stone, protected by palisades. This was where Josh intended to indulge his good mood, alone and on his own horse.

Douglas had to dismount. "You'll get him back when I return," said Joshua, and he leapt onto the pinto. "That's Fort Howard. I don't like the folk there." He really was grinning now.

Absolum was given Douglas's reins, which he reluctantly accepted. Joshua hissed something to his men, checked his revolver, turned his horse, and rode down to Fort Howard.

It was one of those totally pointless raids with neither loot nor any other obvious benefit that Joshua Jenkyns undertook from time to time in order to bolster his reputation, acquire respect, or celebrate a beautiful day. Such acts even frightened his men, who were glad they didn't have to follow him. Douglas motionlessly watched what was happening below, since the view was good and there was nothing else for him to do. It seemed like he was observing a photograph. A wooden castle. Little people. Fort Howard was a long way off, bright and with sharply drawn shadows, as if imprinted into the sunny hollow, a fortress made of light in front of a languid river. One day, thought Douglas, Monsieur Daguerre would surely build a camera that took moving pictures.

Joshua shot two sentries and rode into the courtyard. It all happened very quickly. Men and soldiers, running for cover. Joshua was as visible as a brightly lit target. He shouted and fired, and then fired again. He turned his horse. Shots from his hidden adversaries. Joshua ducked, pulled the horse right around, a blotchy shadow, a blurred image. One final shot and he had vanished.

It had been fun, yet he hadn't thought it through. It was only when he ascended the slope toward Douglas and the men that he realized his mistake. They wouldn't stay put in Fort Howard and lament their dead. They'd come, and they wouldn't delay. Josh had forgotten his hostage, the rider without reins. He had no time to think about that now. The angry men from Fort Howard were already on their horses, and they needed to get away.

Joshua took the reins from Absolum and handed them to Douglas. "Go, mister," he hissed. The riders from Fort Howard were already on their way. Douglas had no time to think either; he spurred his horse to a gallop.

It developed into a grim pursuit. They were barely ahead, and for a long time there was no escape. They rode at an angle to the river, the men from Fort Howard behind them. There were a great many of them. Douglas hadn't forgotten how to urge a horse forward, and he didn't want to wait for the men from Fort Howard. He imagined what was likely to happen if he reined in his horse and shouted: "Gentlemen! Please believe me! I have nothing to do with this!"

Joshua found his path: a hollow, trees, and stony ground. They scattered birds, strange colorful creatures. The path fell and rose again, across a stream and through some rocks. Joshua knew this landscape and its narrow passes. It was a shame that the men from Fort Howard didn't care to follow him here. They would have come one by one, every shot a hit. But the men from Fort Howard knew the landscape too, so they cursed and headed for home.

Joshua stopped and they all dismounted, dusty and covered in sweat. "Oh mister!" said Joshua. "You sure do ride like the Devil!"

"I'm from the country." Douglas swept the hair from his face, having lost the cord that tied it back. He absent-mindedly stroked the horse's forehead, lost in astonishment.

"I always knew it," said Joshua triumphantly.

"Hmm?" Douglas didn't want to speak right now.

"I've known that ever since I met you," insisted Joshua. "You ride like the Devil, and mister, and ..."

"And what?" asked Douglas.

Joshua silently reloaded the revolver.

Jeremy was yelling at the Mayor of St Louis, and had been doing so for half an hour. "Is there no law in this damned wilderness? Is there no police force here?"

"We have a police force," said the Mayor faintly. "Three or four, I believe."

"Three or four what?"

"Three or four companies."

The Mayor tried to explain to the irate Englishman how the police were organized between the Mississippi and the Missouri. They assumed various guises: private, municipal, and employed by the state. There were wealthy people with their own police, there were militiamen and elected sheriffs, and there were also sheriffs who'd been voted out but nonetheless remained in office, much to everyone's chagrin. Jeremy constantly repeated the name he'd learned in Carrolton: Joshua Jenkyns. The Mayor smiled. "Little Josh," he said. "Well, I wish you luck, sir."

The Mayor wasn't the only person whom Jeremy Fortescue yelled at in St Louis. He spoke to lots of people, yet nobody felt responsible. Soon half the town was whispering about the raging foreigner whose brother had been taken by Little Josh for no discernible reason. News arrived of the raid on Fort Howard. No hostage had been present. Josh was riding westward with four men, heading for the Missouri.

This was the only information Jeremy received: Josh Jenkyns is heading for the Missouri. Josh Jenkyns is always heading for the Missouri. The Missouri is Little Josh's great passion.

"I don't give a hoot about Little Josh's great passion!" shouted Jeremy. "I want to find my brother!" People advised him to hire a couple of men and take care of the matter himself. Portland, Jefferson, Booneville—Joshua was sure to pass by there. If need be, Independence. If need be, Leavenworth too. Jeremy would come across him in Leavenworth at the latest.

"I'm not hiring anyone," shouted Jeremy. "I want the damned law!"

Life became somewhat easier for Douglas after Fort Howard. He was allowed to ride with reins, and sleep a little distance apart at night. It was easier with reins, and it was easier to sleep if you couldn't hear Joshua breathing.

Joshua stayed on the pinto. Douglas now rode the horse of the man who'd been shot, but he gave it no thought. Joshua once more remained silent. He provisioned himself with the bare necessities in a desolate village near the lead mines, because they were now entering territory that hadn't yet been populated by settlers.

One evening they were sitting by the fire; Joshua was casting bullets, the men were asleep, and Douglas was scratching his head. Joshua eventually looked up. Douglas was scratching and groaning and scratching. It was bad, certainly mosquitoes, although the Mississippi already lay far behind them. Joshua furrowed his brow. Then he began to laugh. Douglas took his hand from his head and stared at Joshua. Since when was Joshua able to laugh? It sounded unpracticed, a little hoarse, harsh, and self-conscious. He didn't laugh for long. He cleared his throat and then drew his knife from his boot.

"They'll hurt like hell," said Joshua. He held the knife out to Douglas.

"Pardon?" asked Douglas. He didn't take the knife. His head itched a great deal, but he didn't feel like scratching anymore. "Mosquitoes?" he asked tentatively.

"Come on mister, cut your hair off. They're lice. They'll hurt like hell."

"They're not lice!" Douglas said indignantly.

"Sure they are." Joshua stood up, the bare blade in his hand.

"No!" Douglas shouted. Zadock wheezed and pulled the blanket over his ears.

"You gonna do it yourself?"

"No!" Douglas shouted again.

Joshua squatted next to him. "I swear they'll itch like hell," he said, "and you'll be tearin' your hair out by the roots." Then he grabbed Douglas's shoulders, turned him round, and began to cut.

Douglas cried out. Zadock, half asleep, muttered a curse. Joshua cut strand after strand, not too short and not particularly tidy either. "Oh God," whispered Douglas, but offered no resistance. Joshua held him between his knees as if he were shearing a sheep. It felt strange: the knife, Joshua's thighs and hands. The cutting made a curious noise, a sharp blade sweeping through thick bunches of hair, swift and merciless. "Oh God," repeated Douglas. Joshua cut silently, and was soon finished. He replaced the knife in his boot and then sat on the ground in front of Douglas. He looked at him and nodded thoughtfully.

"That ain't turned out so pretty," said Joshua. Suddenly he took Douglas's face between his hands. He pulled his head to the fire and combed his hair with his fingers, to the right and to the left.

"Why?" asked Joshua almost gravely. "Why's your hair got two colors?"

He let Douglas go, painstakingly swept the fallen strands together, and cast them into the fire. It stank. Zadock grunted. Douglas scratched his head in bewilderment, unaccustomed to its lightness.

"Oh," he said. "That's how it is with us Yorkshiremen. The race of Oxnop banshees. Earthbound spirits. We have magic hair. We grow wings if we cut it, and then nobody can stop us from flying off."

"You tellin' me fairy tales?"

Douglas smiled. "My hair is dyed," he said wearily, "and if I don't soon get a little coal tar and chlorinated water you'll one day end up with a blond hostage."

"Hostage?" Joshua appeared to be unfamiliar with the word.

"What's your surname?" asked Douglas suddenly.

"Jenkyns," replied Joshua softly.

Douglas shook his shaggy head.

"But surely your parents aren't of English stock?"

"Scottish," murmured Joshua.

"I don't believe a word of it."

Joshua had pulled a stick from the fire. He poked the embers. "My mother is Omaha," he finally said. "That's why I look like this."

"And what might that be?"

"Omaha."

"Pardon?"

"That don't mean nothin' to you?"

"No," said Douglas, "that means nothing to me."

Joshua scraped at the handle of his revolver with his fingernail.

"Omahas are Indians," he said after a while.

Douglas stared at him for a long time. Joshua gazed into the fire, his hands clasped together. Douglas asked him how old he was. There was no reply. Douglas asked whether he preferred Scots to Indians, and added that the Scots were a wild race. Joshua didn't reply to this either.

"It's awfully nice," said Douglas finally, "that you didn't scalp me, Joshua Jenkyns. Will you tell me why you claim to love me?"

"Because it's true," countered Joshua without hesitation. He fetched the saddle and the blanket. He lay down to sleep. There he lay. Douglas scratched at his disfigured coiffure.

X

JOSHUA CONTINUED TO USE words sparingly. It grew warm-er, and soon it was hot. Douglas placed a hat on his shorn hair, a roughly shaped piece of felt from Absolum's bags. He washed it at a waterhole, though this didn't make the hat any lovelier. Douglas was glad there was no mirror in the prairie. He still scratched at his head. It was better with short hair, but the lice wouldn't go away. At night Douglas would sit silently by the fire like Joshua, his legs crossed, catching them with a look of revulsion on his face and then squashing them between his fingers.

They had long since left any villages behind. The predomi-nant feature was grass. Douglas once tried to ask the man called Zadock where they were heading, but Zadock gawped at him as if he were the Devil incarnate, and made no reply.

Douglas had stopped counting the days, and his watch was no help either since he'd forgotten to wind it. They all had watches, apart from Joshua. Zadock even had four; each of them showing a different time. Nobody ever looked at them.

The salt ran out, and soon there was nothing but unseasoned meat—anything they happened to come across. Douglas ate with equanimity. He was glad when there was rabbit. They often had something rat-like, or those dubious groundhogs that barked in the darkness. Paradise threw stones at them, and Douglas watched him skin them. They tasted somewhat pungent without salt. Douglas's trousers were so baggy that he didn't notice how much weight he was putting on. One evening Joshua observed him for a while and then said he looked like a skunk: two colors, easy to spot in the grass. He once again drew closer in the night, and Douglas gradually grew accustomed to the sound of his breath.

One day at noon, Douglas saw a village or camp in the distance. He pointed at it. Joshua shook his head.

"Wouldn't you like to ride over there with your neat little handgun," said Douglas, "and procure some salt and a bottle of brandy, because I do believe it helps against lice."

Joshua shook his head again. He held his horse right next to Douglas, almost touching him with his knee. Douglas insisted upon his brandy. He was slightly ashamed, but he realized he would have condoned a robbery in exchange for some means of combating lice. After a long silence, Joshua muttered one word.

"Pardon?" said Douglas.

"Mesquakies," repeated Joshua.

"Are they Indians?"

Joshua nodded.

"Are you telling me you're afraid of Indians?"

Joshua looked at him. He grimaced. Suddenly he reined in his horse.

"Come with me, mister. I can't shoot at 'em."

"Me?" asked Douglas. "Why?"

"I can't shoot at 'em."

"Family ties? And what am I meant to do there?"

"That ain't my family," growled Joshua.

"What am I meant to do?" repeated Douglas.

"You," began Joshua, "you, mister ..." He didn't finish his sentence. He took one of Zadock's four watches, ordered his men to wait, and then grabbed Douglas's reins. Douglas muttered something, but Joshua didn't care about that. He slowly led Douglas across the wide stretch of open country.

They dismounted before they reached the camp; Joshua tied the horses to a dead tree. He took Douglas by the arm and pushed him forward. Douglas wanted to free himself, but Joshua held him fast. And so it was that Douglas Fortescue accompanied his kidnapper to the Mesquakies, on foot and armed with a pocket watch, since the revolver was useless here.

There were a couple of tents, together with ragged women and children. Two young men were loading lead onto a cart. They had rifles but bows and arrows too, assembled into a pyramid next to which a woman was breastfeeding her baby. The men with the lead ran off and fetched an old man in a strange costume. He was swaying slightly; he looked sad and the worse for drink. Joshua squeezed Douglas's arm until it hurt. He lowered his eyes in front of the sorrowful old man, who laid his hand upon his chest. Joshua copied him. He hesitated, and then let Douglas go. He pressed the tips of his index fingers together. He rubbed his thumbs together. He scratched his head. Then he formed a cup with his left hand, stirred it with his right index finger, and blew into the palm of his hand. Finally he held the pocket watch out to the old man. Douglas saw it was Jeremy's watch. The old Indian opened it, looked inside, and closed it again. He put it in a pocket on his belt. Then he called to one of the young men and said something incomprehensible. The boy brought salt and a leather pouch. Joshua took it, then ran off as if pursued by the spirits of his ancestors. Douglas was barely able to keep up with him. Joshua ran until they reached the horses. He leapt into the saddle and looked at Douglas imploringly. Douglas mounted and they rode off at full gallop.

Joshua stopped before they'd reached the men. He wiped the sweat from his brow.

"Thanks," said Joshua. He held the leather pouch out to Douglas. "That's medicine against lice, and there's salt, and thanks, mister ..."

"Why are you thanking me?" asked Douglas. "What have I done?"

"You came with me."

"What?"

Josh spurred his horse.

They all received their share of the Mesquakies' lice medicine. Joshua mixed the powder with water and used it to treat his followers. He took them between his knees, one by one: first Douglas, then Absolum, Zadock, and Paradise, energetically rubbing the stinking paste into their hair. He treated himself last. Joshua Jenkyns was a good shepherd.

There was salted meat for supper, a long-legged creature that was extremely oily. The salt made the animal more palatable, thought Douglas. He ate peacefully. The death throes of the lice were unbearable, but then it got better. All five of them sat together, digesting their meal and searching for dead lice. "Aaah," said Paradise, and suddenly began to sing out loud. Joshua grinned. He let him sing. It was only after the third verse that he said, almost amicably: "The Chief was drunk and quiet, and you're sober and loud. That's dumb."

Paradise fell silent. Joshua laughed. And that was the end of the evening's table talk.

Once the men had gone to stand guard or to sleep, Douglas tried his luck again. He wanted to know why he'd had to go with the boy. He wanted to know why Joshua had thanked him. Joshua grinned; he often did so on this particular evening, yet he made no reply. Douglas sighed and wrapped himself in the blanket, relieved about the deathly quiet in his piebald hair. Joshua soon lay next to him. He looked at him for a while, then reached for his hand. He held it, then pulled it and took it under his blanket.

"What are you doing?" asked Douglas.

Joshua closed his eyes. He held Douglas's hand in his, like one holds something—a piece of material, a corner of the pillow—to make it easier to fall asleep. He didn't let go of the hand anymore, and he didn't answer Douglas.

"Am I your talisman, you demented child?" whispered Douglas after a while. Joshua was asleep. He was actually asleep.

"It can't be true," whispered Douglas. He carefully closed his fingers around Joshua's warm hand.

Then Josh smelled the Missouri. He knew this smell so well: water, decay, and something else for which there was no word; if the wind was favorable, he already smelled the river days before he saw it. He hurried his men along. It was hot, the grass was high, but the chief whistled and had to be obeyed.

Douglas couldn't make sense of Joshua's disquiet. He slept alone that night. Josh lay down and jumped up again. He spat into the fire. He ran from the camp, to the horses and back, he took off his coat and put it on again, then took it off once more and also removed his shirt and ran off, stripped to the waist. Douglas couldn't sleep either, and even Paradise grunted, shook off his blanket, and wandered barefoot hither and thither. Josh sat on a hillock, his rifle on his knees, chewed the ends of his headband, and gazed at the sky. It seemed to Douglas as if he was talking to the moon. Soon Joshua ran back to the camp. He oiled his rifle. Then he oiled all the other rifles too. Finally he rummaged in a saddlebag, found a whetstone, and began to sharpen his knife, which he did for hours on end. Zadock rolled grass into little balls which he rammed into his ears.

Joshua was unable to rest on the next night too. When he heard Paradise cursing, he kicked him and sharpened his knife again—an unpleasant noise which robbed everyone of their sleep. Douglas groaned. Zadock was desperately trying to stuff half the prairie into his ears. Paradise attempted to hum himself to sleep. Absolum, who was missing two fingers of his left hand, sucked on the stumps for hours, a pitiful expression on his face. And Josh Jenkyns sharpened his knife till morning came.

The Missouri lay hidden behind scrub and rocks, lethargic, almost a lake, with no current. There were trees here, willows and cottonwoods, some of them bent over and half drowned, driftwood that refused to drift. Joshua ordered his men to unsaddle the horses, then shooed Douglas's horse into the water. He was calm now, almost smiling. Douglas's fine boots that had once belonged to the sheriff of Pleasance were wet. They were the only part of his wardrobe that had survived the journey unscathed. They drove the horses through the water, mosquitoes in their faces. It was deep, then it became shallower, and finally they reached a sandbank from where you could see far across the river in its entire, muddy splendor. "Missouri," said Joshua proudly.

Douglas was unsure whether he liked the Missouri. It seemed putrid and dangerous, a lethargic creature just waiting to pounce. He took in the view, a look of puzzlement on his face.

"Your river, mister," said Joshua at last.

"Thank you. Terribly decent of you. But why is it mine?"

Joshua turned his head and looked into Douglas's eyes. *"A swamp, a river,"* he said gently, *"a muddy brown like coffee ..."* That was all. He caressed his horse's neck and gazed quietly over the brown water. How beautiful it was, here at the mouth of the Grand River!

"I don't believe it," breathed Douglas. "I don't believe it."

XI

J EREMY FORTESCUE TOOK THE steamboat up the Missouri. He stood at the railing, his pockets full of English gold, traveling in pursuit of a law that didn't exist. Jeremy was indifferent to the grandeur of the landscape. He wasn't here to enjoy himself. He left the boat in Jefferson City and went to find the Governor.

"Oh, England, how nice!" complimented the Governor, and amicably enquired whether Jeremy was *au fait* with the art of warfare, as was to be expected from the British, since the days of Admiral Nelson at least. Jeremy snorted. Here too, he asked for the police.

"There are plenty of men," said the Governor, "who would like nothing better than to go with you. They're brave fellows, sir. Take the ones from the mountains. Take the Chouteau boys. They're bored now that the furs have gone, and you'd be doing them a favor. You'd enjoy the Chouteau boys. They box bears for fun."

The Governor laughed, then saw Jeremy's expression and fell silent.

"I'm not Nelson," said Jeremy.

He continued his journey, via Rockport to Booneville. A street, a whorehouse, two Swiss botanists: there wasn't a great deal more in Booneville. There was a sheriff too, but Jeremy didn't like the sheriff. He carried on to New Philadelphia and Chariton. The steamboat passengers had discovered long ago what was driving the fierce foreigner westward. They secretly placed wagers on his life expectancy.

Absolum, Zadock, and Paradise were shooting turkeys. Douglas was sitting with Joshua in the grass, trying to explain something to him.

"I didn't create these poems," said Douglas, "I merely wrote them down." He was undoubtedly saying this for the tenth time, and Joshua was shaking his head for the tenth time.

"Is that your name?" asked Joshua patiently, pointing to the front page of *Colors*.

"Indeed it is," said Douglas, "and I earned some money with the stuff, but I swear it's not by me. Moreover, it's bad. I had to flee England because of these bad poems."

"That ain't true, mister."

"Don't call me mister," cried Douglas. "Good grief! I do have a name!"

Joshua squeezed his eyes tight shut. He was tired. He didn't understand Fortescue. Fortescue talked and talked. He was telling him about a town called London, about foolish people, about books, gossip, and justice. He claimed he'd almost ended up in the penitentiary because of his bad poems, and then he took it back. Fortescue had problems. Josh understood that much. He also understood that Fortescue wasn't familiar with the Missouri. The muddy brown water was a different river. Someone had dreamt it, asserted Fortescue, but not Fortescue himself. Some boy or other had dreamt the river, apparently whilst under the influence, but Joshua didn't properly understand that. "A coincidence," shouted Fortescue, "nothing but a silly coincidence," and he raised his hand, almost as if he wanted to hit Joshua. Then he let it fall again, and groaned.

Joshua didn't believe it was a coincidence. He waited to see whether Fortescue would change his mind. Fortescue didn't change his mind. He spoke a little more about his London, and then he sighed and groaned. Joshua was glad when he finally fell silent. He was convinced Fortescue had dreamt the Missouri himself, and who gave a damn if he hadn't? "I love you," said Josh. He dutifully swallowed the "mister."

"And?" cried Douglas. "And then? And so? What are you going to do about it?"

Joshua gave it some thought. He gazed for a long time over the river. He thought about the time with Fortescue, back then before he had captured him. He thought about the man in the stagecoach, a white cloth over his face. Douglas Fortescue. He rode well and wrote fine poetry. Joshua had told him his secret, but now Fortescue was angry.

"I don't know," said Josh. He looked at the tips of his boots. Fortescue ought to know what to do about love, thought Josh.

"That's the worst nonsense I've ever heard in my life," said Douglas.

He jumped up, ran to the water, picked up some sticks, and threw them in. The Missouri scarcely moved them. They lay still, *half drowned in languid waters*. Douglas picked up stones and threw them at the sticks.

Zadock arrived with a turkey, but Joshua sent him away. He returned Fortescue's books to his bags, then sat down again in the grass. Fortescue had given up throwing stones, and was now pacing up and down by the bank, his hands behind his back. Joshua pulled his knife from his boot. He found a piece of wood and started to whittle. The wood got smaller and smaller, and eventually there was none left. Joshua grabbed the knife by its blade. He aimed and threw. The knife stuck in a tree trunk, close to Fortescue. He was only a little frightened. Joshua wished he'd been standing closer, and that he'd been more frightened. Without turning towards Joshua, Fortescue drew the knife from the tree and found his own piece of wood to whittle.

Evening came, and the men built a fire. They roasted turkey. Paradise sang. Joshua sat as if turned to stone, his chin on his arms. Douglas clumsily sharpened sticks, one after the other, and used them to build a little fence by the banks of the Missouri. Night came. Absolum, Zadock, and Paradise wrapped themselves in their blankets by the fire. Eventually Joshua stood up.

He walked to the horses and fetched two rifles. Then he walked up to Fortescue. He took the knife from him and replaced it in his boot. Then he passed him a rifle.

"Take that," said Josh, "take my pinto, don't ride before sunrise, and ride to the west, not too close to the river, till you see a rock, a cliff. Turn northward there, heading back to the Missouri, and then you'll come to Fort Osage. There's folk there."

"What?" whispered Douglas.

Joshua was silent. He held the rifle in front of Douglas's chest until he finally took it. He gave him ammunition. He turned away and walked off. Joshua chose a place that was close to the water, because he liked the smell of the river. He sat down in the grass again, the rifle over his knees. Joshua Jenkyns stood guard that night, guarding himself and his men. He didn't guard Fortescue. Fortescue was free.

Douglas obeyed in every particular. He saddled up the pinto and set off as soon as the sun rose, the rifle in the saddle loops and Absolum's hat tipped over his forehead. He didn't look round. It was over—a grotesque dream.

For a long time Douglas had just one thought: I need a

barber. He didn't want to think about anything else, and nothing else came to mind. He rode straight, slowly, because he didn't know how far it was to Fort Osage. For the first time he was riding the pinto with reins. It rode well. Douglas tried to forget its owner's name. He couldn't, but he soon would. Douglas Fortescue was a past master when it came to forgetting names. He would find a barber, then Jeremy and the camera, and he would let this horse go, because it looked like it could live without human beings, alone in the wilderness. What precisely was the name of the half-breed who shot people in Fort Howard? No constable; no Jeremy darling. I'll swear he didn't introduce himself.

Independence was dreadful, far worse even than Booneville. Jeremy knew he wouldn't find any help in this town, just a couple of houses inhabited by desperados and lunatics. The people drank and then shot at crows and fences, and windowpanes from time to time too. There was a hotel in Independence where Jeremy had now been living for almost a fortnight, the back of a chair jammed under the door handle because there was no key. Somebody occasionally sent a girl up, which was perhaps well intentioned, but Jeremy didn't want a girl. Jeremy wanted justice, as he had been calling it for a while, because "the law" had started to feel like an alien concept.

Nobody did any cooking in the hotel, but there was a tavern where they cooked meat and beans. Jeremy had to eat, so he went to this tavern and got used to not removing his hat, because that was the custom in these parts. The sheriff of Independence kept him company. He was tired of the jail. Jeremy had found him there in his shirtsleeves, his rifle over his knees, drinking thin coffee in front of a cage where three men and two women were sitting and cursing. He was glad to go to the tavern with Jeremy, even though there was no peace and quiet there either. Nobody paid any attention to the sheriff. Nobody paid any attention to Jeremy. Both of them had long ago ceased to spark any interest.

The sheriff told him about the mountains, about the beavers nobody wanted anymore; he complained about the unrest in Independence, about the trappers who'd become superfluous and who were settling here and misbehaving. He had made his proposal, the proposal they all made: "Equip the men, take them with you, make your own law." Yet Jeremy was pig-headed and probably a coward too, so the sheriff soon gave up.

He told him about a wife and children, about a farm far away in the east that he'd have once he'd been voted out of office, which he hoped would be soon. He recounted heroic deeds from the past. He drank the brandy Jeremy bought for him, and also ate meat and beans. At some point he fired at a man who was shouting too loud, and then took him to the jail.

Day after day Jeremy sat at a dirty table by the window and waited. He soon no longer knew what he was waiting for.

"Go to England," advised the sheriff, "before someone takes your money."

Jeremy shook his head. The sheriff drank. He was no longer young, and had bad teeth.

XII

JOSHUA JENKYNS HADN'T EATEN the previous evening, so he made a substantial breakfast of yesterday's cold turkey. Then he climbed onto a rock and looked at the river. "Fortescue has gone," said Josh to the Missouri. He would have to go to Independence. He needed gunpowder, horseshoes, and flour. He wanted a new horse too, another pinto. Maybe he wanted to rob the bank, even though it certainly wasn't worth it. Maybe it would be fun. Joshua tried to recall the bank in Independence, but failed. He knew where the blacksmith was, the livery stables, the General Store. There was a brothel too. Paradise would find it. If nothing else, Paradise always found the whores. Joshua yawned. The boys had been well behaved; they wanted girls and liquor, and had earned them too.

Joshua looked at the Missouri and polished his revolver. His men were waiting to break camp. Let them wait. Joshua took his time. He sat and polished, and then began to shout. He stood up, fell silent, then shouted once more. The men ducked. Joshua arrived from his rock: a leap, a shout, then merely a growl. The horses were already bridled. Joshua threw the saddle onto Absolum's horse and pulled the straps tight. He jumped into the saddle. The horse bucked and rose up. It raced off as soon as Josh gave it the bridle.

It was almost evening when Douglas heard him approaching. The prairie was burnt here, black countryside with no grass, a great relief for the riders. Douglas didn't turn round because he knew who was approaching. He kicked his horse in the flanks.

Douglas did his best to exploit his head start. It was all over, and it mustn't begin again; no, thought Douglas, you won't catch me a second time. Bent low, he swiftly galloped straight across the black earth. He had the better horse, yet Joshua came closer. Douglas Fortescue didn't look round.

He still didn't look at him when they were neck and neck. He just saw a shadow. Joshua couldn't overtake, but for an instant he stayed close to his prey. Just try to grab my reins, thought Douglas, and then everything happened very quickly. This wasn't a feat you generally encountered in Yorkshire, and it came as a complete surprise to Douglas. Joshua stood up in the stirrups and lifted a leg until he was half kneeling on the saddle, galloping right next to Fortescue. Douglas ducked. Joshua jumped.

When Douglas came to, he was lying on his back, stunned, his head aching. Somebody was saying something he didn't understand. Eventually he realized it was Joshua. Who else. Douglas groaned.

"That'll hurt like hell," said Joshua. "The flies'll get into it." Douglas didn't know what he was talking about. He didn't really know what had happened. His head hurt, and he felt sick. He saw Joshua sitting on the ground, sweaty and disheveled. The picture was blurred. Douglas could see sky, but no horses. He could see Joshua Jenkyns.

"Flies?" he repeated feebly. Joshua pointed to his face. Black fingers. Dust and ash. Douglas coughed. His temple was burning.

"What?" groaned Douglas.

"Grazed, that's all. But dirty like you ain't never seen."

Joshua knelt down. He took Douglas's face between his hands.

"No water," said Josh. "No brandy, no handkerchief." He turned Douglas' head to one side and smoothed his hair back. Then he bent over him and carefully began to lick the dirt from the wound.

It hurt, because it was a big wound: from the corner of his eye to well beyond the hairline. Douglas winced, then kept still. He allowed Joshua to do as he pleased. He felt his tongue, moist, warm, and slightly rough, he felt it slowly moving from one edge of the wound to another, and beyond. It was painful, then less painful. The pain disappeared, together with the nausea. Douglas could also see clearly again, but there was nothing to see apart from Joshua's hair, and it was far too close to form a sharp image.

Joshua went about his business thoroughly. The wound was dirty, and Joshua wanted it clean. It was only when he could just taste blood, no dirt, no earth, that he sat up and looked at the wound. It looked good. It wouldn't attract the flies. Joshua now stroked Douglas's head as if he was also wanting to rectify something here. His five dirty fingers ran through Douglas's tangled and likewise dirty hair. Douglas got used to this contact too, and closed his eyes for a moment. Finally he shook off Joshua's hand and sat up.

Joshua attempted a grin. He failed miserably. Douglas watched him for a while, and then pulled the sleeve of his coat over his hand and used it to wipe Joshua's mouth. He used the other hand to remove the revolver from his belt. Joshua cringed. Douglas roughly wiped dirt and blood from Joshua's lips and laid the revolver behind him. Joshua clenched his fists.

"Why did you do that?" asked Douglas.

"Flies ..."

"What I'd like to know is why you leapt at me like some crazy animal!"

"I couldn't get past you ..."

"A-ha," said Douglas. "Of course. That makes perfect sense."

Joshua was crouching on his heels, every muscle taut. He was shaking. Douglas didn't know whether he wanted to run away or get his revolver, or whether he wanted to leap at him again, or maybe everything at once. He grasped Joshua's shoulders. Joshua grabbed his wrists. Douglas didn't let go. Joshua bared his teeth, unsmiling. Douglas was unable to read his expression.

"Go on," said Douglas.

"I ..."

"Yes."

"Hey, mister," hissed Josh, almost inaudibly. A command. They were too close, their foreheads were almost touching. I don't want to, thought Douglas. I can't. I don't know. He tried to free his hands. Joshua held them fast. Douglas tried again, using brute force. Joshua lost his balance and Douglas somehow caught him, his arm around his chest, his hand on the back of his neck. I don't know! cried Douglas to himself, but he realized he knew very well, and that stopped his breath for a moment.

Joshua turned round in Douglas's arms, on his knees, his hair in Douglas's face. It was almost impossible to hold him, yet Douglas held him; he was heavier, and he exploited the fact. A struggle and yet no struggle, and Joshua defended himself and yet didn't defend himself, and then he defended himself again mightily. He hissed, and tried to say something: "no," or maybe "yes." Douglas couldn't understand him. He grabbed him again and held him fast, and Joshua caught his hands and pushed them away, and then caught them again. It was all a damned muddle: hands and hair and clothes and skin, and the damned prairie, grass and ash, and Joshua's damned belt.

No, thought Josh. Goddammit, and yes, thought Josh. Goddammit, yes. Fortescue behind him, above him, close, far too close, a man, and he himself unarmed—and Fortescue in him, a sharp pain, Joshua bit into his knuckles, and there was Fortescue's hand, and Joshua bit into Fortescue's knuckles, and then he opened Fortescue's hand and placed it where he wanted it, and pain and ecstasy mingled, and Joshua wanted more of it, more of Fortescue, everything, and he said "yes," and Fortescue said "Joshua," and then it was over.

Joshua Jenkyns fell asleep. Douglas could hardly believe it. He fell asleep in his arms, coiled up, his back pressing into his chest. Josh growled whenever Douglas moved, but he didn't wake up. Douglas tried not to move. Absolum's horse came back, but the pinto had vanished.

"Goodness me. And precisely what am I supposed to do with you now?" whispered Douglas. He received no reply. Joshua was sleeping. Douglas would have liked to sleep too, but this was impossible. The arm on which Joshua was lying was the only thing to fall asleep.

Joshua eventually opened his eyes.

"The pinto ain't comin' back," he murmured. "He's gone to

the Devil." He pulled Douglas's arm tighter around himself, and fell asleep again.

"And where shall we go?" asked Douglas. Joshua growled. He wanted to sleep on, preferably until the next morning.

"Where the deuce shall we go?"

"To Independence, to shoe the horses."

"And then?"

"To Leavenworth."

Joshua was almost talking in his sleep.

"A-ha," said Douglas. Then he was quiet. His questions didn't bother him, not now. He gave in to Joshua. He let him sleep and didn't move, so that Joshua wouldn't have to growl and wake up and provide useless answers to equally useless questions.

He left Joshua in peace until his arm had gotten so numb that he could no longer feel it. Then he freed himself, stood up, and pulled Joshua to his feet. Joshua made an effort to wake up. He looked at Douglas in astonishment. Douglas picked up the revolver. Joshua didn't want to take it. He eyed it mistrustfully. "Go ahead," said Douglas. Joshua took the revolver, checked the hammer and cylinder, still half asleep. Douglas smiled.

"Let's go." Douglas pointed to Absolum's horse. Joshua climbed into the saddle, and Douglas mounted behind him.

Josh drove the horse on in silence. They rode slowly back toward the east. It was a bright night and an easy path. Joshua fell asleep yet again. His head dropped to his chest, then he struggled to stay awake, and already he was once again losing the battle against sleep. Douglas eventually reached around him and took the reins from his hand. "Hmm," muttered Joshua. "You're welcome," said Douglas. Joshua leant against him. Douglas held him around the waist and steered the horse.

They reached the Missouri at dawn. The men were already awake, and saw them coming. They were baffled, but kept that to themselves.

"Breakfast," ordered Joshua once he had dismounted, and he was given turkey again, which he ate with a hearty appetite. Douglas didn't want anything. Douglas didn't have to eat. Douglas Fortescue was free.

They set off, towards Bluffton and Independence, on the other side of the river. They rode in silence, Joshua in front. He was riding a spare horse without a saddle, because the saddle had disappeared with the pinto. Joshua suddenly thought of something. He waited for Douglas.

"Now Fortescue's books have gone too," said Joshua. "They were in the saddlebag. That ain't bad, Fortescue, is it?"

Douglas shook his head. "Might you get used to my Christian name, Joshua?"

"Why?" asked Joshua.

"It's the done thing."

"Why?" asked Joshua again. Douglas made no reply. Joshua was silent for a long time.

"I'll try," he finally said. "Fortescue, I'll try."

XIII

J OSHUA DREW ATTENTION TO himself when he reached
Independence. The people here were slow on the up-
take, so Joshua fired into the air. He wanted to stay in
Independence for a while. Nobody would bother him.
Two days, and then onward to Leavenworth. He entered the
main street with his men, Josh Jenkyns' dreadful band trotting
along in single file. The street emptied. Joshua wanted to go
to the blacksmith.

"Get away from the window," shouted the sheriff when he
heard the shots, and gave Jeremy a push. Jeremy didn't want
to be pushed. He was already so familiar with the noise of
gunshot that he was no longer afraid of it. He'd drunk brandy
too; he felt heavy, or light, or both at the same time. Jeremy
remained seated by the window, his hat on his head.

He recognized Joshua immediately. He didn't hesitate because he'd waited too long. Jeremy jumped up, threw the chair

over, then ran onto the street. It was bright, far too bright. Jeremy squinted, then leapt and made a grab for Joshua's reins. He didn't get them. Joshua drew his revolver. Someone shouted: "No!" Jeremy didn't look round. He only saw this boy. Joshua pulled the horse back, the revolver in his hand, and bared his teeth.

"To the Devil with you," whispered Jeremy. Only now did he see his brother, close to Joshua, on a bay horse. He had short hair and an injury to the temple. He didn't look like Douglas.

"Douglas!" shouted Jeremy.

Douglas had grabbed Joshua's shoulder. Joshua resisted, but Douglas held tight.

"Don't you dare," hissed Douglas. "Put the thing away!"

"Douglas!" repeated Jeremy. Joshua lowered the revolver with difficulty, as if his arm didn't want to obey him.

"Go away, Jeremy," said Douglas. It sounded anxious. Jeremy stood rooted to the spot.

"Go away!" repeated Douglas louder. Joshua had shaken off his hand. His horse was unsettled, and the men were unsettled too. Independence wasn't safe, so Joshua changed his plan. He wanted to be away from here. He whistled.

"Please go home, Jeremy," said Douglas, "and get off the street right now."

Joshua pushed Douglas to one side. He spurred his horse.

"Go home!" cried Douglas, then drove his horse to a gallop. Jeremy leapt backwards, and almost fell over. He stared after the riders. Five men and a led horse. He saw dust, sunshine, the empty street, and the rifle in the loops on his brother's saddle.

Jeremy swayed. For a long time he didn't hear that someone was talking to him. Only gradually did he understand that it was the sheriff. "You're crazy, sir, ain't ya?"

Jeremy was still staring into the void. He was trying to understand something. It had happened so fast. He understood something, but he didn't like it, and then he understood nothing whatsoever again.

"Your brother ain't there no more. I sure am sorry," said the sheriff amicably. He hadn't followed the scene properly. He'd stayed under cover. Josh with his men: this was something the sheriff was already familiar with.

"He ain't there no more, your brother," he repeated. "You should head for home."

Jeremy was silent. The sheriff clapped him on the shoulder. Only gradually did it dawn on him what the sheriff meant. "My brother ..." he began. He got no further.

"My sincere condolences," murmured the sheriff in embarrassment.

Jeremy sat by the window again. The sheriff fetched him a brandy. A couple of men shouted "condolences!" and then laughed. Lost his brother and gone crazy. Tries to grab the reins off Josh. More luck than sense. They'd seen half of what was happening outside, but mainly the dust. Did Josh have a new man? There was one, wasn't there? They discussed it at the bar.

Jeremy sat in silence, holding his head. Eventually he heard what the people were drunkenly repeating. Does Josh have a new man? Do we know him? A tall guy. He rides at the front. After a long while, Jeremy clenched his fists and stood up.

"That's not a new man," he bellowed, "that's my damned brother!"

The customers at the bar fell silent. They were familiar with Jeremy's story. Nobody had really seen what was happening outside. The customers thought it was slightly embarrassing not to pay any attention when Little Josh dropped by, and it was also embarrassing and pretty dumb to confuse Josh's hostage with Josh's men. They didn't feel like laughing anymore. The Englishman ought to recognize his own brother. However, the sheriff then looked at Jeremy questioningly.

"The man next to Josh?"

Jeremy nodded angrily.

"I had a different picture of your brother."

"Me too!" shouted Jeremy.

"Tell me sir ..."

"Get me some men," whispered Jeremy. "For God's sake get me some men!"

The town of Independence wasn't easily impressed, but Jeremy Fortescue succeeded. Everybody was talking about the transformation that had occurred in the English mama's boy. Seen Josh and tasted blood! Who would have thought it? The sheriff helped Jeremy to recruit twelve men; there were no more to be found. Jeremy was generous and took the sheriff's advice, since he knew what was customary in such cases. Money up front, plus a bounty: that was best for morale, and of course there was the reward for Joshua too, nicely earning interest in the Bank of St Louis.

Jeremy paid each man his advance in cash. He gave them ammunition, and got the sheriff to check each individual rifle. If he screwed up his nose, Jeremy bought a new one. The sheriff was glad to assist, although he didn't want to accompany him. He lovingly praised the guys the foreigner hired, each and every one of them, as if they were his own sons or horses from his own stable.

Speed was of the essence, since Joshua had gone. News arrived that he was heading for Leavenworth. They had to follow him there. Jeremy compelled respect. The former fur trappers soon obeyed his every word, almost like Douglas's publishers in the olden days, because Jeremy was a talented commander. He bought horses and gave the sheriff the money for the bounty so that he could look after it in his official capacity. He bought himself a horse and a rifle. It differed from the English shotguns. Jeremy shot at crows and hit them. He forgot about Douglas on this horse, with this face, about "go away" and "go home." He remembered the lad in Yorkshire, the poet in London, the photographer in New Orleans, and said to his men: "Gentlemen. Don't shoot my brother by mistake, otherwise there'll be no bounty and it'll all have been for nothing." He described his brother. The man with the two-colored hair.

"Is it a surprise that he hasn't got a barber in this damned wilderness?" shouted Jeremy when the sheriff laughed.

"Your brother ain't no hostage," said the sheriff suddenly. He spoke quietly so that Jeremy's men couldn't hear him.

"Pardon?" said Jeremy.

"He's got a rifle."

"My dear fellow," said Jeremy, "you're dreaming."

Absolum, Zadock, and Paradise had been looking forward to Independence, and they muttered aloud when Joshua changed his mind. They were only hushed when he tapped his revolver, but all three of them pulled a wry face. They'd already been doing so for days. The minds of Absolum, Zadock, and Paradise were slow-moving, yet something was beginning to stir. It was this image: Josh up front in the saddle, and the reins in the hostage's hand. For days on end this image swam around in the minds of the bandits Absolum, Zadock, and Paradise. They would have liked to discuss what it might mean, but they discussed nothing whatever. They silently pulled wry faces.

Joshua had fled from Independence because Fortescue's

brother was there. He was worse than a dozen Indians. You weren't allowed to shoot at the brother, so you had to get out of this town. They found a village where there was gunpowder and a saddle for Josh, and even a blacksmith. Then they set off towards Leavenworth.

Joshua knew he'd have to say something. He wanted to call Fortescue "Douglas," but he couldn't. He looked at him, lowered his eyes, and then murmured: "Fortescue. Ride back to your brother."

Douglas thought about it. Then he began to laugh. "I'm already familiar with that. It's the old story: you'll send me away, give me a head start to make it more fun for you, then you'll show up and jump onto my horse."

"No, I won't," said Joshua.

"Oh yes, you will," said Douglas. He was no longer laughing. They were sitting by the fire. The men were sitting on the other side, well within sight but just out of earshot if one spoke quietly. Josh's henchmen. They didn't dissolve into thin air if Douglas stared at them with his green eyes; he had already tried it. You just had to live with Absolum, Zadock, and Paradise. They were as unavoidable as mosquitoes and the weather.

"I don't believe a word of it," said Douglas. "You won't let me go."

Joshua cleared his throat. "Sure, Douglas. Go to your brother."

Douglas attempted a smile. "Come now," he said wearily. "Take the rifle away from me and tie me to a horse. I'm an Englishman. I've been brought up properly. Do me this favor." Joshua shook his head. Douglas didn't know whether he misunderstood him or whether he didn't want to obey.

"Please, Joshua."

But Joshua just kept on shaking his head.

"Fine," said Douglas after a long silence. "Then don't. By the way: what do you do in the winter?"

Joshua poked the embers.

"Hmm?" said Douglas.

"It's summer now," said Joshua, "and you survive the winter too." He spat. Zadock was cleaning his teeth with the point of his knife. Absolum was sucking wearily on his finger stumps. Joshua stared into the fire. Then he frowned, looked Douglas in the face, and said earnestly and with slight wonderment: "Fortescue. I'd like to do that again."

"I beg your pardon?" said Douglas.

"Yes," said Joshua.

"Goddammit," said Douglas gently. "Be quiet and go to sleep."

Paradise stood guard that night, and his buddies were allowed to lie down. Zadock and Absolum lay next to one another, far away from Josh and the hostage. They snored in harmony. At some point they opened their eyes. Zadock and Absolum looked at each other. They opened their mouths and closed them again, but no words came forth. They stood up and crept across to Paradise. They looked at Paradise. Paradise also opened his mouth, but he was at a loss for words too. What ought they to say? There was nothing to say. They squatted next to one another for a long time, Absolum, Zadock, and Paradise. Then they crept to the horses.

XIV

Joshua's shouting woke Douglas up. "I'll get 'em," cried Joshua. "They won't escape!"

He was standing by the remaining horses, revolver in hand. He was shouting very loud. Douglas pulled the blanket over his head, but sleep was no longer an option.

"The boys have gone," bellowed Joshua. "I'll fetch 'em one by one!"

Douglas sat up. Joshua was still raging. Douglas had never seen him so angry. Josh Jenkyns' dignity as a chief had been sorely aggrieved, and he was incapable of doing anything to save it. Even the spare horse had gone. He had slept too soundly. He had dreamt. Joshua bellowed and Douglas groaned.

Joshua finally fell silent and put the gun away. He trod in the ash, again and again, with both boots. He was quiet now, but he was gnashing his teeth.

"Outrageous," said Douglas. "An impertinence. You really ought to shoot them."

Joshua looked around. Two horses. Grass. Crushed embers and Fortescue on his blanket. He was getting blonder and blonder, a skunk in his summer coat. Joshua snorted. The boys had gone. Fortescue was smiling.

Jeremy reached Leavenworth with his men, but Josh wasn't there and hadn't been there either. He'd had a considerable head start. He ought to have arrived ages ago. Jeremy's men were familiar with the area, and they said there was no reason to linger between Independence and Leavenworth.

Jeremy didn't want to wait again, but he had no choice. Nobody knew where Josh had gotten to. Had he turned around? Had they overtaken him? Jeremy's men said that was virtually impossible. They were at a loss. They thought about the bounty. Would he still come? They were almost giving up hope. What could have held him up? There wasn't much apart from grass and the Missouri between Independence and Leavenworth.

Joshua Jenkyns had been dawdling ever since that morning when Absolum, Zadock, and Paradise had bid him farewell. He was angry, and remained so for an entire day, but he made no attempt to carry out his threat. Josh let the men go. He rode in silence, with a fierce expression. It had become very hot, and even Joshua was now obliged to wear a hat, a shapeless affair that was tied firmly at the back of his neck with a piece of cord. He pulled the brim down low. He rode in his shirtsleeves, at a very leisurely pace. Douglas rode with him and observed him.

Douglas Fortescue observed Joshua Jenkyns riding throughout the length of a warm summer's day. This activity required Douglas's full attention. He didn't know what had happened to his eyes. He was unable to get a sharp image. The finely ground lenses of Fortescue the photographer had become dull, or had broken when he'd fallen from his horse; they were no longer reliable. Just as Joshua struggled with his anger, Douglas struggled to regain a clear view and a clear head: fervently, half-heartedly, defiantly, and yet with rapidly weakening powers. He sought words for what he could see—for the strangely blurred image of a boy who rode worse than a peasant, let alone an English gentleman: with slack reins and slouching shoulders, his boots dangling carelessly in the stirrups. Douglas could find no words to describe this image. He continued to observe Joshua through his maladjusted eyes, observed Joshua Jenkyns' crude riding skills, his damp shirt and his dogged expression, his eyes that were shaded by his hat, the beads of sweat, and the very black and not very dense fuzz on his upper lip. *I'd like to do that again ...* They maintained a resolute silence. *Yes Joshua, me too, here and now!* Douglas squared his shoulders and tightened his reins. They rode without exchanging a word until evening came.

Joshua fired. They still had enough provisions and it was far too hot to hunt for supplies, but Joshua fired all the same. He shot at birds with his rifle, killed them, and left them lying on the ground. Then he found a tree with wild plums, where he several times emptied the cylinder of his revolver, shot after shot, plum after plum—the awesomely steady hand of Josh Jenkyns. Douglas observed this too. He wondered why Joshua did it. Maybe he needed to sort something out in his head. After all, Douglas knew that Joshua used his revolver to sort lots of things out—why not this too, whatever it might be. Douglas didn't ask him. Joshua fired until the mood had passed, then reloaded and grinned. "Better now?" asked Douglas. Joshua nodded. Slightly embarrassed, he spun the revolver around his finger, then tucked it into his belt.

It didn't cool down that evening, and it didn't cool down during the night either. They ate in silence, followed by yet more silence. Joshua had cleaned his guns and cast his bullets, and was now playing with them. Douglas heard them click in the hollow of his hand, again and again, a high-pitched clicking, almost like the mechanism of a clock.

Suddenly Joshua said, "Thank God!" Douglas didn't know what he meant. He heard himself say, "Yes, Joshua, thank God!" This conversation didn't make the night any cooler. The bullets clicked. Douglas scratched at the scabs on his temple. They occasionally looked at one another, and then for a long time could do nothing else. It was very still; only the tiny creatures of the dark scratched and crackled in the grass. There wasn't much air to breathe that night by the Missouri. Joshua eventually lay down to sleep. Douglas eventually lay down to sleep. The sleeping wasn't a great success. They had to wrap themselves tight in the blankets because of the mosquitoes, and it was far too warm. Joshua propped himself up on his elbow and looked at his hostage again. He gently bared his teeth. He was saying goodnight: Douglas interpreted that correctly. He watched Joshua coil up and pull the blanket over his head. Maybe he was sleeping. Maybe he wasn't. Nobody stood guard that night; Joshua had the revolver in his hand.

He didn't find any reason to hurry on the next day either. Douglas suspected that he'd long been following a zigzag course, but he didn't mention it to him. Joshua knew the land. Douglas was the captive. Admittedly he did have a rifle, but he still played the hostage. This hostage wasn't desperate to reach Leavenworth either.

They came to a stream. Joshua wanted to water the horses and bathe. He ran barefoot for a long way through the scrub, and finally undressed. "May I bathe too?" shouted Douglas. There was no reply. Joshua crouched silently in the water behind the bushes. Douglas undressed. The stream was cold, but it felt nice. The cold didn't last long.

They rode in a zigzag throughout another hot day, and a second long night passed. Douglas admired Joshua's healthy appetite. He'd hardly woken up before he started to eat: cold meat from the previous evening and those abominably hard dough cakes that he baked with a passion. "It ain't coolin' down," said Joshua. "No," said Douglas, "I'm afraid it isn't."

By noon that day Joshua was finally riding so slowly that Douglas's horse became unsettled. They briefly looked at one another. They dismounted and unsaddled the horses in unison, and without saying a word. It wasn't a pleasant spot. The sun was burning down, the grass had long ago turned brown, and two scrawny trees provided scant shade. Joshua tied the horses up. Then he walked into the sun and just stood there, hat tilted back. His countenance was fixed, almost expressionless, and yet suddenly easy to read.

Douglas obeyed. He walked the couple of steps that separated him from Joshua, who was standing there waiting, utterly transfixed as he was sometimes wont to be, a familiar and yet puzzling image. And the closer Douglas came, the more puzzling and less familiar this image seemed to him. He hesitated. He felt he ought to greet Joshua respectfully, formally, just as one greets an opponent before a duel. But Joshua was tired of waiting. He leapt at Douglas, who caught him informally in his arms.

Joshua quickly broke away again, and stepped back. Then he undressed from head to toe. Douglas also obeyed in this respect. He struggled with the tight boots that had once belonged to the sheriff of Pleasance; for a moment he struggled with himself. His hands were brown, and his body white. And too wide and too tall. And hair everywhere. Douglas slowly straightened up. Joshua stared into his eyes. Then he looked him up and down with obvious interest. Douglas lowered his gaze. He took a hesitant step, and this time Joshua caught him.

Joshua wanted many things and everything at once. He wanted to hold Douglas and wanted Douglas to hold him. He wanted to close his eyes and yet didn't want to be blind. He wanted to stand and fall, fight and surrender, he wanted the terror, the delight, the pain he had already sampled, and the ecstasy he had hitherto only glimpsed, he wanted all of this immediately and yet he wanted it to last for minutes, hours, until the end of the world—the desires of Joshua Jenkyns were mightily confused, and he sighed or hissed because he didn't know whether he wanted to sigh or whether it would be better to hiss, and then Douglas heard him draw breath, deeply, as if he were preparing for a fight.

Douglas played at fighting with Joshua. He maintained his composure. He wanted to know what it felt like: what he was doing with Joshua, what Joshua was doing, what they were doing together, with one another, against one another, for one another, all at the same time. He wanted to know how to control the game, how to yield to it, how to urge it forward and rein it back in. Douglas looked into Joshua's face; he smoothed his hair back and grabbed it again and held it fast, because now he wanted to look into his eyes. And Joshua once more drew a deep breath and had to sigh, which he did, and he wanted it so much, he wanted to do it with Fortescue, precisely that, precisely so, eye to eye. And he wanted it to go on. He wanted it to last, to last until he could no longer bear it.

It lasted for a long time. They were good at this. The sun shone impassively and the crows kept on flying. They didn't frighten the horses. The world remained as it had been, an indifferent world composed of grass and two trees, somewhere by the Missouri.

But then it could last no longer. Douglas saw that from Joshua's look. He recognized something about this look. He knew what it meant. Yes, Joshua. Do it. Let me hear it. And Joshua shouted. He let forth his notorious cry, which often frightened himself, the cry for his lack of words, for friends and foes, for the lawless country; the cry for the poems he didn't understand, for the love he didn't need to understand, the cry of bewilderment and triumph and joy. Joshua shouted. It didn't frighten him, and it didn't frighten Douglas either. Douglas remained silent. Joshua shouted for the two of them. Douglas bit his lips. They had reached their destination.

It was a long time before they managed to collect themselves. Joshua chewed his knuckles for minutes on end, lost to the world. He lay motionless, held so tightly that it almost hurt. He was very warm and very wet. Douglas absent-mindedly traced his fingers over his back, over the sharp outlines of his shoulder blades, rapt and not fully awake. The sun burned down mercilessly. Finally Joshua took his fingers out of his mouth and cleared his throat several times.

"That was," said Joshua, "that was ..." He faltered. "I mean," Joshua began afresh, slightly hoarse and almost outraged, "that was ... I mean, you ride and then ..." Joshua got no further. He sat up. He grinned. "Then all of a sudden you unsaddle the horses in the noonday sun, and then ...*mister* ..." Now Joshua had lost his self-composure. Dumbfounded, he shook his head and began to laugh in a way Douglas would never have thought possible. He laughed until tears ran down his cheeks. Douglas kept his mouth shut, but to no avail. Soon he was laughing with him. Soon Douglas could no longer stop either.

"We gotta carry on," said Joshua when he'd caught his breath.

"Leavenworth?" asked Douglas.

"Hmm?"

They tried to laugh again, but the moment had passed.

"Just get into the shade," said Joshua. "Leavenworth can wait."

XV

THEY DIDN'T TRAVEL ANY faster after the midday that turned into a night. Douglas and Joshua made the most of the time they'd been given. Leavenworth, Josh knew, was the last settlement. There was nothing north of Leavenworth, only the Missouri. There was nothing to the west, just land, and then the mountains. Indians lived there, hunters. They didn't dig lead like the sad Mesquakies. Joshua reeled off their names to Douglas: Kanza, Delaware, Pawnee. They were of little concern to him. Joshua didn't want any dealings with the Indians. He still had gunpowder, and he even had some flour. Above all, Joshua had his hostage; he was more than happy to deal with Fortescue.

"Nobody'd ever guess ..." said Joshua. "Nobody'd ..." He looked at Douglas for help, but to no avail. "Goddammit ..." began Joshua again. "Nobody ... goddammit, ain't nobody'd ever guess that!"

"And nobody can do it as well as us either," said Douglas.

He grinned. Joshua pondered, then nodded earnestly.

It was night. They were tired. They had learned to sleep with one another. Nobody stood guard. They slept peacefully, Joshua's cheek on Douglas's chest, Joshua's hand on the revolver.

The miles that separated Independence from Leavenworth doubled. Douglas's watch stood still. The grass stood high. The sun stood in the sky. Now and then Josh uttered a couple of words from a poem into the surrounding countryside, as if that was where they belonged. Joshua had always done so when he was traveling, and he wasn't terribly bothered when Douglas winced. Eventually Douglas didn't wince anymore. The words sounded strange when Joshua said them, and strange in this country. Yet maybe this was really where they belonged. Maybe the whole of America was nothing but an Englishman's belladonna-induced dream.

"So long as it's not *Thirst*," wailed Douglas. "After all, it's hardly fitting!" Joshua grinned. He recited a couple of lines of *Thirst*, very slowly. He savored it. Sometimes he relished his poet's discomfiture. "Sure it fits," said Josh. "Blood for sure, and thirst too if you don't plan things right."

He cleaned and oiled his guns. Douglas watched him repeatedly spin the cylinder of the revolver, play with the hammer, and trace the engraving: *Samuel Colt*—earnestly, almost lovingly. Douglas derived pleasure from this, though he didn't know why.

Days later, Joshua issued the command. It came suddenly. "A-ha," said Douglas. "Leavenworth," repeated Joshua. Douglas nodded. Joshua was probably right; it had to happen. They set off.

Two men were watching out for Joshua Jenkyns, although people hardly believed he'd come anymore. There was just one route from the northeast to Leavenworth, and he would come from the northeast if he came from Independence. So this is where the lookouts hid, playing cards for days on end.

Everything had been prepared for Josh. Jeremy enforced discipline. Day after day he repeated the same sentence: "Don't shoot at my brother." Day after day he thought less about the meeting in Independence. He remembered how Douglas's hands had been tied back then on the road in Illinois. He remembered Josh. "I want the boy. Dead or alive," he said, then shuddered.

The men were urging him to depart. Go back toward Booneville; he's turned around. Then one of the lookouts arrived. Josh was on his way, alone with the hostage. The hostage had a rifle. "Nonsense!" cried Jeremy. He shouted for his men.

Joshua realized as soon as the first shot came. He saw Douglas rein in his horse, and knew it was too late. Joshua was familiar with Leavenworth, and he was familiar with traps. This trap was bad. Josh spurred his horse.

Douglas didn't understand, but he obeyed. Heads down, they galloped straight along the main street. Douglas heard the shots, the whistling of the bullets. He saw nothing. It was dusty. They were close to one another, Josh and the hostage, and that put the marksmen off. They fired all the same. They'd waited a long time. They wanted Josh, even at the price of this Mr Fortescue whom they weren't supposed to shoot at. Soon there was nothing but dust. Jeremy's men emerged disappointedly from the houses. Little Josh had gone.

Joshua rode hard towards the west. He could hear Douglas next to him, but he didn't look at him. He knew they would follow him right away. They were the men Douglas's brother had recruited, because he'd seen the brother. He was foolhardy. He didn't take cover properly. He had over ten men, well armed. Josh had two rifles and his revolver. He had two horses for two men. He had enough gunpowder and far too little lead. That was the situation.

Joshua found his narrow pass, drove his horse between the rocks, then dismounted and led it up between the scrub and the stones. Douglas was there, following him. Joshua still refused to look at him. Finally he stopped and took both rifles.

"Your brother sure is angry," said Joshua.

Douglas stared at him. He had by no means grasped what had happened: shots and dust, so suddenly, and now it was over.

"Your brother has roughly ten men."

Douglas only slowly came to his senses. He saw Joshua standing with two rifles under his arm, dispassionate.

"My brother?" whispered Douglas.

"That was your brother. Go talk to your brother."

Douglas made no reply. "My brother doesn't shoot at people," he finally murmured.

"Go to him, Douglas. Go talk. He'll be here any minute."

Joshua unsaddled the horses and led them into the bushes, under cover. When he returned he could see the riders. Douglas thought about Jeremy, what Jeremy was or wasn't doing. He no longer knew. He had been sorely deceived about himself; why shouldn't he be deceived about Jeremy?

"So what am I supposed to say to my brother?" asked Douglas. Joshua shrugged. He couldn't help him.

"I don't want to," said Douglas.

Joshua nodded. "Get down. The cover is bad."

He made a rampart out of the saddles. Douglas lay on his stomach and hid his face in his hands.

"Don't shoot at my brother."

"No."

"Will you recognize him?"

"Yes."

Joshua opened fire as soon as the men were in range. He hit a horse with his first bullet, and its fallen rider with the second. Douglas saw Jeremy; his horse reared, he fumbled with his rifle, shouted a sentence that Douglas couldn't understand. The men headed for cover behind their horses, and fired. Their bullets hit rock. One hit Douglas's saddle. Joshua reloaded, the tip of his tongue between his teeth. Jeremy was still shouting. Douglas wanted to shout back "go away" or "come here," but he didn't. Joshua fired. Now Douglas took the rifle and reloaded, just as Jeremy had once taught him in Yorkshire. Joshua accepted it without looking. He hit a second man. Then the men in the posse turned around. They would come again, from the other side, and send two men in the night to fetch their dead. Joshua was familiar with all this. It was the same old game, always the same. It had been fun once, but it wasn't fun now. Joshua stood up. They couldn't stay here. He checked the rifles and the revolver.

"He has four children," said Douglas. "He wanted to buy land in Illinois. He always takes care of me ..." He fell silent. Joshua wanted to go back to the horses. He paused and looked around him. He looked tired. Douglas was frightened to see how tired Joshua looked.

"We'll get out of this," said Joshua, "and then your brother can go back to his family."

"How do you mean—out of this?"

"Just keep goin'."

"And then?"

"Head west." Joshua took hold of Douglas's shoulder and urged him forward.

It was a long journey. Joshua did as he'd been taught. Douglas did as Joshua ordered. They didn't speak much. They rode westward, day after day. Jeremy's men dared to come within range on two further occasions, but they came off worse. The posse stayed on Joshua's heels, and he knew he couldn't escape them. They were trappers from the mountains, and they read his tracks like a book. Sometimes he recited a couple of lines in the night, when he longed for a fire and roast meat; a couple of lines of Fortescue, or occasionally some Byron too. Douglas pretended to sleep. Joshua watched him for a long time. He stroked his hair, which was almost blond now. The brother was completely blond. Sometimes, when he was very tired, Joshua thought he ought to creep back at night, on foot, and capture Douglas's brother and explain everything to him. The brother would let them go once he understood everything. After all, the brother was the brother. This is the kind of thing Joshua thought when he was very tired. He spat and sniffed. Sometimes Douglas would then sit up, take the rifle, and let him lean against him.

Jeremy leaned against his horse. He was tired too. In one week he had lost six men. People said he was too impatient. You needed to starve Josh out and keep him away from water, and not run in front of his muzzle. They hastily and impassively buried their comrades, but they wondered if Jeremy had lost his mind. He wanted to catch up with his prey, to free a brother who loaded Josh's rifle for him; everyone had seen that long ago. "Me too," shouted Jeremy. "He's mad. Don't shoot at him!"

"Give up," said Douglas. "Sit and wait."

Joshua looked at him, then looked toward the west once more.

"I can't," said Joshua, "and you don't want to."

Douglas was silent.

"I still have one bullet," said Joshua. "They say the last bullet is lucky. I don't know why. But I'll save it."

They reached Solomon's Fork. You couldn't see the river. The ground rose, and they had to lead the horses. Joshua knew this place because he had already been here once, but he no longer knew why. The Santa Fe trail? Was that here? Had someone died here, someone with silver? Joshua couldn't remember. He knew they had to climb: a cliff, with the river far below. The Kansas River was blue and filled with rocks; it had long since ceased to be the Missouri. They needed water, but they wouldn't get any here. They carried on climbing, then Joshua shooed the horses into the scrub. They reached the highest point where the rocks were steep, almost concave. Just a moment ago Josh had had a plan. Now he no longer knew why he was here. The riders had almost caught up with them, and Joshua could hear them coming.

"You can't get down there," he said. He was tired and hungry. Douglas was far better at going without food, but he was tired too.

"I don't want to go on," said Douglas. He sat down. Now he could hear the riders too.

Jeremy's men knew about this cliff. A good view for Josh, hardly any cover, no way out. He's reckless, said the men, he's gone crazy. They caught Douglas's horse and reluctantly marked time. Nobody wanted to go up there.

Jeremy was tired too, and didn't want to go on either. "Stay here, gentlemen," he said, then dismounted and took his rifle.

Douglas and Joshua stood up when they heard him coming.

"We could jump," said Joshua.

"The Devil we could," said Douglas.

They waited.

Douglas and Jeremy briefly looked one another in the eye. Jeremy didn't want to talk to his mad brother. He wanted the boy. He aimed. Douglas made a move. Jeremy fired, and hit the wrong man.

Joshua took a closer look. He was familiar with this. He knew precisely what it looks like when a man falls and then doesn't get up anymore. He wanted to obey: not the brother.

He couldn't obey. He gave Jeremy his last bullet.

Jeremy Fortescue died before he had time to comprehend it: a shot between the eyes, as Joshua was wont to do. Douglas had more time, but he couldn't comprehend it either. He saw that Joshua was sitting next to him with a fixed expression, the revolver in his hand. Douglas knew him so well; it was comforting. He wanted to draw breath. He couldn't. The light was too bright. Douglas closed his eyes.

Joshua silently laid his hand on Douglas's cheek. It felt strange. He took his hand away again. He looked at Douglas questioningly. Was he angry because of the brother? He wasn't angry. He was almost dead. Joshua touched his cheek once more, and this time he left his hand there.

He heard the men coming. He didn't want to move.

"I ain't got no more bullets," said Joshua.

He slowly rose to his feet. He saw the brothers lying there, still and serene, as if they'd already been lying this way for a long time. They resembled one another, the strange brother and the so familiar friend. Joshua wanted to shout, but it was no good. There was no cry for this. Joshua looked at his empty revolver. Joshua looked at Douglas Fortescue for the last time. He turned towards the river. "I'll try, Douglas," said Josh Jenkyns to the Kansas River, and then he jumped.

CHRISTINE WUNNICKE lives in Munich, Germany.
She has published four award-winning novels, a biography,
translations, as well as both documentary and literary radio
programs. *Missouri*, first published in Germany in 2006, is
her first book available in English.

DAVID MILLER has translated many books from German
to English, including the graphic novel *Roy & Al* by Ralf
König. He lives in Newcastle-upon-Tyne, UK.